DRAKE'S HONOR

MADELINE MARTIN

PROLOGUE

July 1342
Lochmaben, Scotland

The sun was beginning to set as Greer MacPherson finished the last of the few days' collection of washing. But where was Mac?

She glanced over her shoulder as she plunged her hands into the icy barrel beside the river, expecting to see her younger brother bounding over the hill with his usual youthful exuberance. He'd seen twelve summers with an unfettered joy she had never been afforded, and that was exactly what she wanted.

She'd wash all the clothes in Scotland if it kept him innocent and happy.

The water in the barrel was cloudy from lye soap that stung at her chapped hands, but she edged around the familiar discomfort and fished out a kirtle—the last item to be washed. After a practiced dunking in the quickly flowing water of the river, she rose with the broad basket clutched in her hands, the weight of the wet clothing making her tired arms quake.

Normally, she would gather the garments from the line that had been dried by the sunshine earlier and hang the sodden clothing straight away. Except a gnawing at the back of her mind made her set the basket down inside the door of their cottage and follow the well-worn path to the meadow.

Where was Mac?

He loved the meadow, aye, but he'd always returned by early afternoon. If nothing else, his bottomless stomach had him sniffing about the large clay pot where their bread and cheese were kept from vermin.

The breath huffed from her lungs as she made her way up the hill, the tension in her chest there by nerves rather than exertion.

Something was amiss.

She reached the meadow as the late afternoon light took on a reddish hue. "Mac?" Her voice carried on the wind, unanswered.

She ran through the tall grass and stopped short when she came across a figure on the ground. Not Mac. Thanks be to God.

But Greer's relief was short-lived.

The woman lay prone, face up and pale against the verdant lawn, her neck cocked at an unnatural angle, her golden hair loose and snagging over the grass about her like fine cobwebs. Her blue eyes were open, wide as they stared sightlessly upward.

Her gown was precious silk, a pink that turned orange in the strange light of the setting sun that twinkled at the gems on her neck.

Greer took an instinctive step back. Finding a dead noble was never a rewarding deed for a peasant. That was when she caught sight of the small wooden hoop laying on its side; the one Mac loved to roll through the grass.

Icy dread tightened in the pit of her stomach. Suddenly, she had an idea of where Mac had gone. He would not have quietly left such a scene. Nay, his kind heart would have compelled him to find someone to help. Someone who would take him prisoner for what he'd found. Or worse...

Greer spun on her heel and fled the meadow, heading straight for Lochmaben Castle, and prayed to God that her brother had indeed been taken there. Then at least, there would be an opportunity to have him released.

And she would do anything to see her brother safe.

August 1342
Dunfermline, Scotland

D rake Fletcher's dream was within his grasp. He approached the dais, his head held high in the presence of the young monarch who might forever alter his life.

"We hear ye are an honest man," King David said from where he sat upon a massive carved chair in the Great Room of Dunfermline Palace. Sunlight streamed in through the cross-hatched windows and caught at the gilt thread on his fine crimson tunic. "Yer brother-in-law, Reid, recommends ye most highly. 'Tis why we've summoned ye, as ye're well aware."

Drake drew in a deep breath. The room was warm, heightening the clean scent of the rushes beneath, freshly changed and strewn with meadowsweet and lavender.

"Aye, sire," he replied.

"Lord Androll's eldest daughter, Lady Eileen, has been found dead." The king spoke in a voice low enough not to carry through the open space to where a servant stood by the closed door. "Androll refuses to believe her neck was broken from a fall and instead suspects a nefarious deed. As he is one of our closest advisors, we would be remiss to no' look into the matter further."

The king sat upright to retrieve the chalice from a small table beside his ornate chair. "Lord Calver is a most lucrative supporter of the crown and has been asking for a guard to help train his men. We'd like ye to go under the guise of assisting him while ye uncover what happened to Lady Eileen. We suspect it might have been one of his soldiers, mayhap a lover's quarrel." He lifted a shoulder. "If ye discover the truth of what befell her, we'll see ye knighted."

Knighted.

Drake's heart thudded hard at the word. His father had been a knight, a man of great honor. As a boy, Drake had looked up to him every day until the fateful battle where his da had been slain. As a man, Drake had aspired to become just like him.

It was no simple task to become a knight, however, when one's father was of English birth and one's mother was Scottish. The mixed blood in Drake's veins had made his path that much harder. It also made the king's words now that much sweeter.

What was more, it was the perfect time for such an opportunity. All three of his sisters had settled into married lives, now safely away from the border between the two countries. Even his mother had moved to the Highlands when Clara, the gentlest and kindest of them all, decided to move to the Isle of Skye with Reid, who she had recently wed.

Drake would never stop worrying about his family, but at least now, he knew them to be protected and well cared for.

Now he could truly focus on his dream.

"I accept the task," Drake replied. "Indeed, I'm honored to be considered."

The young monarch rubbed his chin under his short beard. "What say ye to a squire?"

The question took Drake aback. Squires were not offered to men who had not yet been knighted. It was far too great an honor to bestow upon him.

"Forgive me, my liege," he spoke carefully, loathing the words he had to drag from inside him. "I couldna accept a squire without being a knight."

"Ye *are* honest." The king chuckled and motioned to his servant at the side door. The man was older with a pate that shone through his cottony white hair. He disappeared at once, knowing exactly what was wanted.

"The lad is a bit overeager and..." King David tilted his head in consideration. "Mayhap moral to a fault. We think some travel will do him good."

Moral to a fault?

Was such a thing even possible?

Regardless, Drake was relieved to know of the lad's integrity. No doubt he would be little trouble. "If it pleases ye, Majesty, I would be honored to travel with the lad."

The door to the side of the Great Hall creaked open, and the old man returned with a small boy. Far too young to be a squire. The lad's skinny legs were like twigs beneath his tunic as he hurriedly approached the dais.

"This is Beathan, but everyone calls him Bean." The old man put his hand on the boy's shoulder and turned to him. "Ye'll be traveling with Master Drake Fletcher, aye?"

"Ye mean Sir Drake." The lad shook his thick brown hair from his brow and peered at Drake with piercing blue eyes.

"He's no' a knight," the king replied. "Yet."

Bean's left eye squinted with his apparent confusion. "But why—"

"The travel will do ye good, lad," the servant said encouragingly.

The boy didn't attempt to hide his pout as they were dismissed from the Great Room. Drake didn't take offense, knowing all too well how lads could be, and instead led him out to the corridor.

"Where are we going?" Bean asked, rushing to keep up with Drake's long strides.

Drake slowed his pace somewhat. "Lochmaben Castle, to help train the earl's guards."

"I hope ye're taking him with ye," a stout man said as Drake passed. "And that ye'll be gone for a long while."

Whatever question Drake might have asked died on his lips as Bean seemed to shrink in his skinny frame.

"Farewell, Bean," a squire called from beside a well-dressed knight. Both laughed with a cruel, mocking tone.

Drake narrowed his eyes, but before he could say anything, Bean spoke up quickly, "Are we leaving now? I'd be fine if we were."

"Whenever ye're ready." Drake continued to focus on the knight and his squire with his hard gaze.

"I was informed I'd be leaving today and had time to prepare," Bean replied efficiently. "Though I did expect to be traveling with a knight."

Drake couldn't help but smirk at the second reference to his inadequate rank and guided the lad away. "Forgive me for the disappointment."

Bean swept the hair from his eyes with a hard jerk of his head. "Ye seem fine enough, and I know King David wouldna ever put me with someone unkind. He's always liked my da." He eyed Drake's sword. "Maybe ye could teach me to fight? My da said I wasna ready yet, but that was last year."

Drake regarded the boy, assuming him to have seen ten summers or so. Far too young to be trained with a sword. "Mayhap in a bit."

Bean opened his mouth to protest, revealing his two front teeth, overlarge by comparison to the others. "I'm no' as young as I look. I'm four and ten."

"Of course ye are." Drake swallowed his surprise. "I only meant I wouldna let someone use my da's blade. We'll need to procure a weapon for ye."

There was certainly truth to that. The sword had protected Drake's da in battle for years and was the only thing Drake had inherited that he hadn't been forced to sell. Even in those stark years following his da's death, Drake hadn't been able to bring himself to part with the beloved weapon.

"Go on and collect yer things." Drake nodded toward the stairs that crept upward into the cool darkness of the castle. "I'll be in the courtyard."

Bean gave a single, firm nod and dashed in the opposite direction while Drake made his way out of the castle. He'd never enjoyed being inside, especially on a day so fine as the August one that greeted him with open sunshine and an endless blue sky overhead.

A woman in a plain dun-colored kirtle swept past, her long auburn hair falling down her back in a thick rope of a braid that bounced against her bottom. Drake slid his gaze away, not wanting to ogle.

Instead, he put his mind where it belonged—on the mission at hand, on the details he knew and those he would need to gather. He'd never been tasked with unearthing a murderer before, not like this. For certes, he would need his wits about him.

He wouldn't have looked back at the young woman again if the sensation of being watched hadn't settled in a heavy presence over him. His gaze flicked up, and he found the woman glancing over her shoulder at him, her green eyes sparkling, and her mouth curled up at the corner in a flirtatious smile.

A bonny lass, to be sure.

But there were many bonny lasses in this world and only one opportunity to become a knight.

Drake directed his attention back to the castle entrance as he waited for Bean to return, determined to keep from being distracted by a woman. After all, he knew the dangers of beautiful women and how loving them could wreak the greatest kind of pain.

❦

THE KING HAD REFUSED TO SEE GREER. IRRITATION RANKLED her. She was exhausted from her long travel and her stomach gurgled around the discomfort of its mean emptiness.

The guard back at Lochmaben Castle had confirmed Mac was within the bowels of their dungeon. He swore he knew nothing of why her brother continued to be held but had agreed to help so long as she offered a bribe of fifty marks.

It might as well be fifty thousand.

She'd hoped to find assistance with the king for her unjustly incarcerated brother, but the royal guards had taken one look at her and turned their pert noses up before sending her away.

Fifty marks it was, then.

She glanced back toward the dark-haired warrior she'd passed near the castle. It was his sword that first caught her eye as she exited the castle. Fine quality steel, solid and well-made. It would fetch a nice bit of coin.

The man was well-made himself with broad shoulders that spoke of a muscular physique and the kind of square jaw and intense dark eyes that commanded attention.

He'd looked at her once before, but any additional attempt to catch his notice was ignored as he returned his attention to the castle without interest.

She turned away with a shrug. It didn't matter. There were plenty of people about with costly goods on their person, items that would be easier to slip away with than a large sword.

Indeed, she'd never seen a crowd such as the one loitering before Dunfermline Palace. The men and women wore silks and brocades that cost more than the sum of all the money she'd ever had in her lifetime. Gold and silver adorned their throats, ears and hands, with gems winking in temptation. Greer assessed them all with a critical eye, gauging their worth.

Even with several fine pieces, it would take a considerable number of pilfered effects to amass the required bribe.

She paused in her assessment to deliver a scowl in the direction of the castle and hoped the chill of her glare somehow reached the heart of the king. Or at least the men who kept her from seeing him.

She was a nobody. She knew that. A woman in a homespun kirtle absent of any embellishments. A woman who might have been better off being an orphan than to have had the da she'd been cursed with. He'd cared more for drink than he had for his children.

Aye, looking at herself by comparison to the nobles lingering about in their costly attire, it was no wonder she wasn't shown to the king when she'd sought an audience.

Usually, she could convince people to do nearly anything. It was a gift. Her father had deemed it such once, his skinny chest puffed up with rare pride. Which, of course, meant the skill was an immoral one, like the incredible deftness of her hands.

Everything she had ever been good at was wrong. Frustration simmered low in her stomach. Mayhap that was why living an honest life for so long had been so damn hard.

Though she'd not taken in laundry for over a month in her travel to Dunfermline, her fingers were still cracked at the creases from so many years of working with the harsh lye soap. Honest work didn't pay.

Especially not fifty bloody marks.

Mayhap it truly was to her benefit that she was good at being bad.

Her abilities might be the only thing to keep Mac from certain death.

She had a way of standing out when necessary, with a confident gait and a toss of her rich, auburn hair. But she also knew how to blend into a crowd, slinking low into herself and tucking her head down.

Different situations required different responses. Now, in a thick crowd of so many watchful gazes, she did the latter. Her shoulders hunched forward as she rounded her back, reducing her average height to a more diminutive stature.

A woman standing nearby wore a shimmering green silk gown, a sign of great wealth. Or at least once upon a time, it had been. Now the hem was dimpled with stitch marks from being let out, and the band of her wide belt had shifted, revealing an old stain. The woman might have had fortune at one point, but now she appeared to be enduring hard times.

Greer turned from the woman for a new target, one who didn't appear to need every coin on their person.

Several guards clustered together a few feet away, and Greer shifted her direction again, away from them and toward a lone man who stood by with his purse looped carelessly over his belt.

Easy pickings.

Her pulse didn't so much as tick offbeat as she steered toward him, her gaze fixed determinedly on something beyond the man as if walking with stalwart intent. She'd done this before, count-less times, when stealing was her only opportunity for coin.

It had meant the difference between life and death on many occasions. Not only hers but also Mac's.

He'd been so small, a bairn of only two, when their mother had walked out on them. There had been no food, no milk and their da was as useless as the tail on a pig. That had been the first time she had stolen but was certainly not her last.

The man didn't notice her now as she approached, his atten-tion combing over a wealthy noblewoman some feet away.

Perfect.

Greer swept by him, her fingers nimbly slipping the strings of his purse from their loose hold and easing the treasure into her waiting palm. And what a treasure it proved to be. Its weight was significant with the promise of wealth. In a smooth, practiced motion, she curled her hand back toward her to secret the purse away as she strode purposefully toward the edge of the crowd.

"My purse," the man cried.

She didn't quicken her pace or try to shrink deeper into herself. Nay, that would give her away. Instead, she continued as she was, though her heartbeat did kick up a notch. It wasn't until she turned behind an inn that the panic quickening through her system eased.

"It was ye." The voice came from her right, sudden and harsh with accusation.

She startled to find the man approaching, his face tense with rage. He followed her into the alley, cornering her where she'd meant to shelter, and put his hand on his wide hips, mouth frowning beneath his dark beard.

Greer widened her eyes, feigning an innocence that always served her well, and held up the purse. "Was this yers? I saw it on the ground and—"

The flat of his hand cracked against her cheek, sudden as a snake striking. She reeled in surprise. It wasn't that she hadn't been struck before, for she certainly had been. Rather, people usually offered an alternative before resorting to violence.

Malice glittered in the man's cold eyes. He would get his purse and his revenge all at once.

The alley ended in a wall behind her with no way out but past the man. Greer cursed her poor choice in location for her attempt at refuge. She ought to have known better.

He stepped toward her, drawing his arm back once more as she slipped the dagger from her pocket. She couldn't kill a nobleman, or she'd be dead herself, with Mac soon following. But she could scare the cur into thinking she might.

Before she could even show her blade to her aggressor, a shadow swept into the alley. "I wouldna lay another hand on the lass if I were ye." The voice was low and calm, the threat in the tone more evident than if the warning had been bellowed.

The man turned once more to Greer and she caught sight of the man who had rescued her. A smile pulled at the corners of her lips.

He was none other than the man with the fine sword who hadn't appeared at all interested in her. Mayhap he wasn't so uninterested after all. And mayhap she could use that to her advantage.

2

I f the man were not of noble birth, Drake would have slammed him to the ground the moment the knave laid hands on the auburn-haired lass. As it was, Drake being a commoner, paired with his hope of becoming a knight, placed him in a precarious position.

Men who struck women and children were the lowest sort and ought to be subjected to the strictest punishment. He only wished he could be the one to mete it out.

The nobleman glared at Drake first and then Bean, the man's haughty gaze assessing, no doubt tallying worth in an instant. In an instant, he assumed Drake's fine tunic made him as noble as all of the others parading in front of the palace, and the man pointed an accusing finger toward the woman. "She stole my purse."

The lass's green eyes were bright as sea glass and large against her slender face. She blinked. "I dinna take it. I found it laying on the ground next to him—"

The man's upper lip curled as if he finally could smell the reeking piles of refuse littering the sides of the alley. "Lies."

The woman's pleading gaze swept to Drake. "'Tis true."

It wasn't. He'd grown up with three sisters and knew the look of feigned innocence when he saw it. While he didn't condone lying, the red mark on her cheek encouraged his sympathy toward her. Even if she had stolen the purse as the man claimed, she did not deserve to be struck.

Drake folded his arms over his chest. "If the purse belongs to him, return it."

The woman cast her focus to the purse. It was for a blink of a moment, but the longing there was palpable enough to strike Drake in the chest. One need only take in her coarse homespun dress and lack of adornment to know she did not have much to her name.

Still, she extended the small leather pouch to the man, cradled like something precious in the cup of her palm. Her fingers were split at the creases, and it made Drake recall his own mother's hands. She'd taken in laundry from neighbors and strangers for years to keep them all fed. Her own hands had appeared thus, worn and beaten down by the abuse of a hard life.

The man snatched his purse and stalked from the alley, muttering obscenities as he did so.

"Noblemen shouldna use such speech," Bean chastised, earning him a glower from the man. "And ye could offer yer thanks."

The nobleman tossed the lad a rude gesture, but Drake ignored him and went to the woman to assess her injury.

"Are ye well?" he asked, approaching slowly.

Those wide green eyes found his, and her chapped fingers went to her cheek where the skin bore the imprint of the man's hand. "I've had worse."

He didn't doubt it. Life was hard for women of little means with no one to protect them.

Drake indicated the inn. "Will ye join me for an ale and some food?"

She lowered her hand from her face and studied him. Her

assessment was different than the nobleman's had been. She didn't weigh him for wealth but for danger.

At that exact moment, Bean approached. "My lady, I pray ye are well."

Her mouth pulled up in a tender smile. "Ach, I'm fine, lad. But thank ye for thinking of me."

"I hope ye've offered aid to this elegant lady." Bean regarded Drake sternly.

Before Drake could speak up, the woman replied for him, "Aye, he has. Can I trust him?"

Bean twisted his lips in thought before responding, "The king trusts him, and therefore so do I. He seems a good sort from the bit of time I've known him, my lady."

"And how long have ye known him?" the woman asked.

"Less than an hour, my lady."

The woman gave a good-natured laugh and ruffled Bean's hair, receiving a besotted smile in return.

"Aye, I'll join ye," she said. "But ye need no' call me a lady. Just Greer will do well enough."

Greer.

It was a short, simple name for a woman who appeared to be curiously complex even in the scant time Drake had known her.

"And ye can call me Drake," he said.

She nodded and allowed him to lead her toward the inn where the tavern was known for its lamb and vegetable stew. Once Greer's attention was off Bean, the lad swiftly raked his hands over his hair to smooth what she had rumpled as he trotted after them.

The tavern was relatively empty when they entered, the hour too early to draw in a large crowd. Drake found a table in the corner near the open shutters. The slight breeze wafting in took the edge off the thick air that reeked of stale alcohol, sweat and oily tallow candle smoke.

The tavern maid approached them with a bright, friendly

smile. "What would ye like?"

Drake waited for Greer to speak first.

But it was Bean who began ordering before them all. "I'll have lamb stew and a loaf of bread. Do ye have a bit of cheese back there as well? And an ale."

Spoken as a growing lad.

Greer pressed her lips together, appearing hesitant to order. It was a scenario Drake was far too familiar with—being surrounded by food and starving for lack of coin to purchase any.

"We'll take two stews and ales," he said for her. "And another loaf of bread to ensure this lad doesna bite our hands if we try to have some."

Bean regarded him with horror. "I wouldna ever do something so crude."

But Greer gave an easy laugh, and the offense relaxed from his features.

During the time they waited for their food and ale to arrive, Drake learned she was not from Dunfermline and, like them, was beginning the start of a journey.

"Where are ye going?" Bean asked.

"Back home," she replied without specification. "And ye?"

Drake understood the immediate question, one meant to gently shift the topic from her by putting it back on the other person. Given people's propensity to discuss themselves chiefly, it was an effective tactic. But one Drake did not miss.

"We're traveling to the border to help train soldiers to defend Scotland better." Bean's thin chest lifted with pride. "They need strong warriors."

The tavern maid appeared with their food and ale and set it all on the table before them. The thick gravy sent curls of savory steam up from the trenchers, and a light foam frothed over the ale. Drake hadn't been hungry before its arrival but now found himself famished.

Greer tore a chunk off the bread with delicate care. Though

her actions were measured as she dredged the soft white insides of the bread through the stew, he caught the slight tremble of her fingers and the way her eyes closed when she put the food into her mouth. It was brief, but Drake was suddenly glad he had insisted on buying her meal. She had evidently not eaten in some time.

❧❧❧

THE LAMB'S MEAT WAS SO TENDER THAT IT PRACTICALLY MELTED against Greer's tongue. She tried to maintain a casual air as she ate but wished nothing more than to cram each bite faster into her mouth. She'd subsisted on meager rations of ale, stale bread and cheese to preserve as much of her coin as possible. In the sennight she'd been in the village trying to gain an audience with the king, she had finally run out of coin and hadn't eaten anything in two days.

Now that she had food—a proper, hearty meal—she wanted to be chewing and swallowing even as she was bringing more to her lips. It took nearly everything in her to slow her pace.

Especially when Drake's eyes were trained so carefully on her. She ought to have been disconcerted by how clearly that he seemed to understand her. But there was something fascinating about the way he read her so easily—he had a story of his own to be told, no doubt.

And one she didn't have time to learn.

It was kind of him to purchase her meal and ale, but with the exception of that quality sword on his hip that she'd like to sell, she had no more use for him or the lad. Not when Mac awaited her.

She glanced up at the boy and found him working a piece of the stale bread trencher free before popping the bit into his mouth. A line of foam showed on his upper lip from where he'd drank deeply of the ale.

She lifted her brows. "Ye've quite the appetite."

"Beathan." He wiped his mouth with the back of his sleeve. "My name's Beathan. My da always says the same thing, but he says 'tis good for a growing lad. And I'm hoping to eat enough to grow as big as Drake."

Drake nudged aside his own empty trencher. "Everyone calls him Bean."

The boy scowled. "I dinna like being called Bean."

"Ach, but Bean is a fine, playful name," Greer said encouragingly to put him at ease. She tousled his soft hair the way she did so often with Mac.

The action pulled at her heart and brought to the forefront all the thoughts she'd tried so hard to push from her mind.

Was Mac being well cared for?

Was he safe?

Was he scared?

No doubt he was terrified, wondering when she would come for him. Already she had taken far too long. The trip to Dunfermline had not been easy when done on foot, especially with limited means. Likewise, the return journey back would be equally as long.

She wished she could snap her fingers and be there with Mac in a moment's time.

"I dinna mind if ye call me Bean," the lad said, bringing her back to the present and drawing her from things she'd rather not ponder. He flushed and gave her a besotted smile.

"Where did ye say ye'd be traveling?" Drake asked.

Greer studied Drake, unable to help the rise of suspicion. In her experience, someone asking where she intended to go was seldom an innocent question.

"South," she answered simply.

"We're heading down that way as well," he said. "Ye're welcome to join us if ye like."

The rise of suspicion became a spike.

Ah, so this was how it was to go. Rescuing her, offering a meal paid with his coin, then a generous suggestion to travel together. She was no fool. She knew what came next.

Men didn't do anything for a woman without expecting a display of appreciation. One that they were not shy about trying to exact when not given freely.

And it would never be given freely. Even for a man as fine-looking as Drake was. She'd never been that kind of lass.

Nay, she would stick to her nights on the cold ground before she would accept the "generosity" of a rich man.

Suddenly, she wanted to steal his sword and did not feel a lick of remorse for her intent.

"Please say ye'll join us." Bean's sky-blue eyes lit up with excitement.

She paused, considering. If they thought she meant to join them, it would present an opportunity to sneak away with Drake's sword. "Aye, mayhap for the day."

"We intend to leave once we are finished here." Drake surveyed the table of empty trenchers and mugs.

"That was also my plan." Greer stood up, eager to encourage the start of the journey. The sooner they departed, the sooner they would be alone, and she would have the opportunity to relieve him of his sword.

She could practically feel the weight of coin from its sale in her purse. It would be considerable indeed.

Together, they went to the palace stables where Drake and Bean both had horses. Yet another boon that would prove beneficial for her. If she could take one of their horses as well, she could reach Lochmaben in only a couple of days rather than the weeks it'd taken to arrive. Once there, she could sell the animal for more coin. Between the sword and the horse, she would be well on her way to securing Mac's freedom.

"Where is yer horse?" Bean asked her.

Were he not so serious, she might have laughed. Clearly, he

had no idea the cost of a horse and how many months of food that might otherwise purchase.

She shook her head. "I dinna have one."

"No' everyone has a horse, Beathan," Drake replied.

At the use of his full name, Bean grinned despite the light chastisement. It was a kind consideration. Drake indicated his steed and looked to Greer. "Ye can ride with me."

She hesitated. Bean's horse was little more than a pony that could doubtless only carry the weight of one person. Drake's destrier, however, was a beast meant for war, the kind that could withstand a warrior's weight as well as that of another person and more.

Except that Greer and Darke would be pressed close together. Her stomach clenched with dread for any accidental brushes of his hands with them being in such proximity.

Mac.

The reminder of her brother steeled her resolve, and she acquiesced. Drake helped her up first. The massive horse sat higher than any of the few she'd ever ridden and made it seem as though the world were smaller from her vantage point. An unexpected heady excitement swept over her.

The large warrior swung up behind her, and she tensed in preparation for the heat of his groin settling against her bottom. But it did not.

Instead, he shifted slightly in the saddle, not moving nearer but farther away. He smelled pleasantly of something clean and spicy, tinged with the quality leather he wore at his waist and on his feet. When his arms came around her to take the reins, he did not once brush against her. Nay, he kept his touch removed from her person as he issued a soft click and his war horse began to walk alongside Bean's steed.

Greer's heart hammered with uncharacteristic anxiety. Usually, she was able to maintain her confidence, free of the jitters of her actions. Why then was she suddenly so very nervous?

❦ 3 ❦

Drake remained stiff in his saddle, where he perched precariously, as far back as was possible. Anything to keep his distance from Greer.

He'd caught sight of the way she looked at him when he suggested they share his destrier. Unease.

He was not ignorant to the ways many men treated women, especially the lasses of little means. But most importantly, he was a brother, someone who had over time learned the inner thoughts of women, confessed to him by his sisters in moments where they sought his counsel. In the years he had been their confidante, he had compiled that learning into a great list in his head to ensure he always demonstrated utmost respect when it came to women.

And in this case, that meant keeping his body from touching Greer's.

He was glad she had joined them. The way she had eaten continued to play out in his mind, her hands shaking as she brought the food to her lips, her throat swallowing too fast despite the measured pace with which she chewed as if she could not consume the food quickly enough.

It troubled him to imagine her on the road, traveling without protection, hungry and without shelter. For surely, if she could not afford food, then she certainly could not afford an inn for the night, which left her at the mercy of the elements and exposed to the possibility of attacks. There were expenses for her care that he could gladly see to in an effort to assist her home safely.

She put up a strong front, of course, wielding a shield over her emotions to keep anyone from getting too close. Save Bean, who gazed up at her with the undeniable twinkle of adoration. But there was something vulnerable there within. It was buried deep but appeared in subtle flashes in her eyes: a glint of wariness. It woke in him a need to protect her.

She was too slight despite her fiery spirit, her body unable to keep up with the strength of her determination.

Rage simmered through him when he thought back to the nobleman who had struck her. What would he have done if Drake had not run him off?

The sun was still high in the sky when Drake suggested they stop. It was far earlier than when he ordinarily would have paused for a respite, but he suspected Greer was not used to riding for several hours on end. A brief break would most likely do her good. His back could use a reprieve as well if he were being honest. Holding himself rigid for so long left a jabbing pain in the lower area over his hips, and he couldn't wait to walk it loose.

They located a spring before halting their steeds and sliding to the ground. Drake helped Greer from the horse, careful to touch only her hand and not reach for her waist, even when she stumbled slightly upon landing on unsteady legs.

She regained her balance and gazed up at him, her long-lashed green eyes beautiful and sunlit in the summer afternoon. A smattering of light freckles dusted the bridge of her nose and the tops of her cheeks. Her lower lip was fuller than the top one, and Drake was hit with the sudden urge to run his tongue along its plumpness—to sample the taste of her mouth.

He turned away abruptly and clenched his hand into a fist to squeeze away the unwanted desire. "I should gather wood."

"Are we making camp here?" Bean asked.

Drake shook his head. "Nay, but there's a good bit of tinder about," he replied brusquely. "I'll gather some now for tonight's fire."

Without waiting for Bean to reply, Drake strode off into the surrounding woods with intent. Too late, he realized he'd left his sword behind. He wouldn't go back for it. Not now, when his temptation for Greer was so great.

He hadn't known where that lash of desire had come from. The lass was appealing, aye, and triggered in him a need to protect. But that was as far as it ought to go. He shouldn't have the urge to study her mouth, the desire to kiss her.

There was only one other time he had felt thus...with one other woman...

He drew in a deep breath and closed his eyes.

Immediately, Anice came to mind. Long, curling blonde hair, innocent blue eyes, her beauty otherworldly. And not meant to be his.

She was happily married, and he'd been glad to see her thus. She was a good woman who deserved only the best in life.

He only wished it hadn't caused him so much pain.

His life had no room for romantic entanglements. Drake had long ago set aside his own happiness to see to his sisters and mother. And now that they were safe, he could ignore his longing for a family of his own a little longer, at least until he had earned the title of knight.

There would always be time for love later when he was ready. After all, wasn't that how love was best found?

GREER STOOD ROOTED TO THE SPOT WHERE SHE'D DISMOUNTED from Drake's horse. He had been almost formal when he'd helped her down, but there was something in the way his gaze had lingered on her face. There was interest—enough that she thought for half a moment that he might kiss her.

The realization hadn't been met with dread but with a little flutter in her stomach. A curious reaction, not one she normally had towards men. And a reaction she was not inclined to explore.

She was simply here to gain access to his sword and horse before fleeing to get to Mac faster.

She turned from the horse and found Bean staring at her, a slight flush coloring his cheeks.

"Ye're no' going with him?" she teased.

Bean looked after Drake with a frown.

"Ach, I was only jesting." She winked at him and strode toward the narrow stream to splash the dust from her face. The water was cool against her gritty skin despite the otherwise warm day, and she breathed in the scent of damp, rich earth.

It would be far easier if Bean left, but she knew better than to be so obvious in her suggestions.

"In truth…" Bean pursed his lips. "I wasna going with him to gather wood, but I do have a need to wander from camp a bit. If ye dinna mind."

He squirmed with his legs pressed together as his cheeks deepened to a mortified red.

"Nay." Greer shook her head before his embarrassment could overwhelm him. "I dinna mind in the least." She waved her hand. "Off with ye."

He gave her a grateful smile, reminiscent of the ones Mac so often sent her way that the force of it struck her directly in the heart. Bean scampered off, wandering through the tightly packed trees until he was out of sight.

This was her chance.

She rushed from the stream to where the destrier was still

strapped with the saddle holding Drake's sword. He'd gone into the woods without it. She'd noticed it as soon as he'd left, half expecting him to come back to reclaim it.

This was all too easy. Nothing in her life had ever been easy.

She glanced about before scrambling onto the high back of the destrier. In one swift move, she could be gone with his bag, his sword and steed. She lifted the worn leather reins and clicked her tongue.

The horse didn't move.

She tapped her heels to its sides.

Still, the horse didn't move.

Wasn't that the way of getting the beast to trot onward? By clicking one's tongue and tapping their heels against the great velvety bellies?

She'd never owned a horse to know what to do. It looked simple enough, but the beast refused to abide by her commands.

Damn.

Sweat ran down her back, and urgency pressed at her. Drake and Bean would not be gone long. She didn't have time to trifle with a stubborn horse.

Jumping down from the massive beast, she plucked Drake's sheathed sword from the saddle. She moved to grab his bag and stopped. He had been kind to her. She couldn't leave him with no coin, no food.

Leaving his bag in place, she hustled to Bean's small horse, hopped on its back and clicked her tongue. The petite, compliant animal strode forward without hesitation. Granted, the beast wouldn't fetch nearly the price a destrier would, but travel would be far faster, and whatever she could sell it for in Lochmaben would be beneficial. Every bit of coin would be needed.

She'd watched Drake's movements guiding his own horse with a careful eye in the hours they'd ridden and applied the same motions now. That she was able to navigate at all was most likely due to the mount's gentleness and less to do with her own inade-

MADELINE MARTIN

quate skill. But she still managed to wind her way through the woods, not back the way they came or even in the direction they'd headed, but to the far right.

Her heels tapped the beast's sides, and the pace quickened to a trot that jarred her where she bounced in the hard saddle. It would not take long for Drake and Bean to realize she'd gone, nor to realize what had been stolen. They would, of course, be chasing after her.

Sunlight dappled her path as she squeezed between trees whose slender trunks grew almost too close to one another. Perfect for a pony, but a deterrent for a destrier. Mayhap would save Drake from catching her as his horse could travel far faster than hers otherwise.

Seconds crawled into minutes as she waited for a shout behind her. It did not come.

The forest began to thin, and in the distance were several curling billows of smoke. She had found what she'd been seeking: a village. She could approach a blacksmith to sell the sword, then trade the pony and a bit of the coin for a faster horse and be on her way without Drake and the lad any wiser.

Guilt rose in her gullet, an unwanted emotion when she had so little choice in the matter. Its discomfort, however, was ebbed away by the mere thought of Mac, alone in a cell, dirty, hungry and scared. He was waiting for her rescue.

The poor were never well treated by their lords, especially not when they had been perceived as a criminal.

"Forgive me," she said under her breath to the two from whom she'd been forced to steal, wishing the balmy summer breeze would carry her words back to those she had so wronged.

Before they could catch up with her, she urged the horse toward the village and prayed she might soon have Mac back home.

❦ 4 ❧

A pile of slender, dry sticks gathered in the crook of Drake's arm when Bean's voice pierced the air with the crack of adolescence.

"Master Fletcher," the lad shouted. "Hasten back!"

There was an urgency to his tone that had Drake dropping the wood to the ground as he sprinted back to the horses. Bean stood by Drake's destrier, his head swiveling about, searching the surrounding forest.

"She's gone," he cried.

Drake relaxed, realizing the lad was merely upset about Greer having gone on her own path. "Some travelers prefer to be on their own way. I'm sure she dinna mean offense."

"But she took Brevis."

Drake tilted his head. "Brevis?"

"My horse." Tears shimmered in Bean's eyes. He clenched his jaw and slid his gaze away. "My da let me pick him out..."

A swift glance confirmed the pony was missing. Drake hissed an exhale.

"We can track her, lad..." he started, then stopped abruptly as his gaze landed on his saddle. And the very apparent absence of his sword.

His stomach curled into a cold ball of ice. His father's sword. The only thing he had left of the man he had so loved and admired. It wasn't often Drake cursed, but he did so now at the loss of such a treasured possession.

"A knight shouldna ever utter such coarse language," Bean said miserably and turned his bright blue gaze on Drake. "But I understand."

"Ye're right. I shouldna have said what I did," Drake conceded. He put a hand to the lad's shoulder and squeezed it. They both had lost much that day. "Come. We'll see if we can find her."

Drake helped Bean onto the destrier, then swung up behind him. From that vantage point, it was easy to make out the paths on the field where horse hooves had trod, leaving the grass flattened. One in the direction they'd come. And one to the right, disappearing into the forest.

No doubt she was heading toward the nearest village to unload the horse and sword. Even if they did not find her, at least they could reclaim the things that meant so much to them. Recovering them would be costly but worth every groat.

Drake guided his steed in the same direction and immediately began to follow her trail. It was easy to do so with so many broken sticks and twigs. The lass did not know how to travel discreetly. As they traveled, the trees became dense, meaning they had to navigate more carefully and at a slower pace, which made the press of urgency enough to drive Drake mad.

Bean gave a sniffle from where he sat in front of Drake. "It was cruel of her to steal from us. Especially after we had shown her such kindness."

While Drake's reaction had been a flash of anger with a similar line of thought, he had enough experience with thieves to know their deeds were seldom done for pleasure. Especially female thieves, who had so few options available to them by way of earning an income.

Again, the yearning to protect Greer caught him in a hard grip. He could still recall the way she had regarded him with such wariness when he'd offered to let her ride his steed with him. That immediate need to distrust was not innate; it was learned. And oft through hard experiences.

"Ye dinna know what circumstances can lead to such desperation," Drake replied.

"Stealing will always be wrong," Beathan said vehemently. "My da says ye should always respect the belongings of others."

"Aye, and he's correct," Drake agreed. "But mayhap she needs help."

The lad went silent at that, thinking over what Drake had said.

Snapping twigs and the dull thump of the horse's massive hooves thudding into the soft soil filled the lack of their conversation. In the distance, several streams of rising smoke indicated a nearby village. Tension knotted in Drake's shoulders.

Hopefully, he was correct in his assumption that was where Greer had gone.

"We should offer her aid." Bean's voice cut into Drake's thoughts. "If we find her."

"Ye'd aid someone who stole from ye?" Drake asked, surprised at the lad whose thick voice indicated he was still aching from the loss of his pony.

The slender shoulders in front of Drake lifted in a careless shrug. "If I'm able to be reunited with Brevis, it doesna matter, I suppose. And if the lass is in trouble, wouldna it be our duty to offer her aid?"

"Aye," Drake answered slowly. Bean wasn't incorrect. But then, Drake also had an obligation to ensure Bean stayed safe. What if the lad had tried to stop Greer from leaving? Would she have hurt him?

He recalled her demeanor with the boy, how she'd ruffled his hair like a child, and reserved her brightest smiles for him.

Nay, she wouldn't have hurt him. Or at least, Drake didn't think so.

But was he willing to stake the boy's life on that assumption?

The scent of smoke grew more apparent as they arrived at the village's edge and mingled with everyday odors of village life, where pigs walked about in the alleyways and refuse piled up. They slowed as they passed the simple huts on the outskirts and worked their way inward to the center. Multiple stalls had been set up for market day.

"Of all days, it had to be market day." Bean's proud posture deflated somewhat.

Granted, the multitude of people in attendance would provide more of a crowd for Greer to blend into, but Drake knew it would be impossible to miss her. Not the wealth of her auburn hair bound back in a braid or the slender waist and generous hips he couldn't keep from noticing, no matter how much he tried not to.

She was not a lass he would ever overlook again.

He scanned the surrounding area, seeking Greer or Bean's horse or even the blacksmith's shop as he suspected.

Urgency pressed in on Drake, nipping at the edges of his patience.

Not only to save his sword and Bean's pony, but also mayhap the woman herself.

THE BLACKSMITH'S SHOP WAS A STONE STRUCTURE WITH A SLATE roof. The door was propped open to reveal a glowing forge and a figure moving within. Greer tied Bean's horse to a post out front and strode into the shop. A large man in a leather apron was bent over an anvil, a bit of glowing red metal secured in a pincher grip by a pair of tongs. Catching sight of her, he set aside his hammer and the tongs and straightened with a grin.

His gaze moved appreciatively, first over her, then over the hilt of the sword where it jutted from its leather-wrapped sheath. She pulled it free and tried to make its weight appear easily managed with one hand.

It wasn't, though. The solid metal seemed to weigh more than a millstone and left her arm trembling with the effort to hold it aloft. She set the stolen item upon the stone counter as slowly as she could despite her eagerness to be free of its heft.

If the blacksmith noticed her struggle, he didn't make a show of it. Instead, his gaze danced over the weapon from hilt to tip. "'Tis a fine sword."

She tilted her head up at him. "Worth a fine bit of coin, aye?"

His pale gaze lifted to hers and his eyes narrowed. "Is it stolen?"

She gave a carefree chuckle. "Does it matter?"

"Aye," he said sternly. "It does. 'Tis an arming sword, one belonging to a knight, I wager. I'll no' have a knight up my arse for buying his weapon."

Damn.

A shop owner with a conscience was no friend to a thief.

"Well, I'll no' trouble ye then." With a nonchalant lift of her shoulders, she reached for the hilt.

The blacksmith put his hand over the weapon, trapping her fingers between the heat of his rough skin and the cool metal. "This sword doesna belong to ye."

The seriousness in his eyes told her any attempt at arguing would be a losing battle. It was time to change tactics.

She widened her eyes, letting them soften with innocence. "Please let me leave," she said quietly. "I'll starve if I dinna have this."

The furrow of his brow melted.

"Please," she whispered. "I've no' eaten for two days." It was a lie this time but hadn't been on many other occasions. She would say anything to leave the shop without being dragged to the local lord and thrown into the dungeon.

There would be no helping Mac then.

The very thought caught at her heart and made it flit about like something wild and trapped.

The light in the shop dimmed as the entryway was blocked. "That sword isna for sale." The familiar voice sent dread thumping in Greer's chest.

Drake.

Panic whipped around her. There was nothing for it now. She would be thrown into the dungeon, like Mac. And they both would be left to their dismal fates.

An image flashed unbidden in her mind of Mac cold and hungry in a dank cell, wondering when she would arrive to help.

And now, she never would.

The men she was up against were just and honorable, both far larger than she.

She might be able to run. The possibility stuck fast in her mind and set her heart racing. She spun about with intent and found Drake directly behind her.

Usually, she was swift with a ready quip, an excuse, anything. Now, she simply stared up at him, her breath coming and going so fast, it made her vision go dim. "I…"

His expression was hard, his mouth set in a firm, thin line. "Did ye have the blade sharpened?"

She blinked. "I…"

"She was trying to sell it," the blacksmith offered. "I take it this sword is yers."

"Aye, 'twas my da's." Drake continued to look at her as he said pointedly, "'Tis all I have left to remember him."

He said it in a reverent way that indicated his father had been one worth remembering. Unlike her own, who had been found stone-cold dead on the doorstep of a tavern four years prior, a jug of spirits clutched in his stiff hands.

"I asked her to have it sharpened, no' sell it." He gave her an easy smile that made the guilt inside her burn as hot as the blacksmith's forge.

"Will ye sharpen it?" Drake pressed the man.

Greer turned around and regarded the blacksmith.

The man looked first to Drake, then to her, his eyes narrowing perceptively before running his finger over the edge. "'Tis already sharp."

"I want it sharper," Drake replied.

Still, the man hesitated until Drake reached into the purse at his side and withdrew a coin.

Greer could not help but let her gaze linger over the fat pouch of coins. What must it be like to always have ready access to funds? To never worry about where one's food would come from or where one would sleep that night? The unfairness of it ached inside of her and filled her with a spiteful ire.

Drake would never have to face a brother whose life could only be saved with thievery. He'd never known hunger or struggle.

The blacksmith accepted the payment, took the sword, and pressed his foot down on a petal that set a large grindstone spinning.

Greer didn't know why Drake appeared to be helping her, but she had no intention of staying to find out. As soon as the blacksmith set the sword to stone and the scream of sharpening metal cut the air, she slowly stepped backward.

"Beathan is waiting for ye outside," Drake said in a casual tone. As if he had anticipated she would attempt to leave.

Damn. No doubt she would receive her punishment in other ways. Would Drake insist she repay his kindness with servitude? With her body?

Her stomach tightened.

At least it would not result in her being locked in a dungeon where she would not be able to save her brother.

She would bear anything to ensure she remained free to save him.

Bean waited outside for her as Drake had promised, the flat of his hand braced against his brow to block out the glaring sun, his other hand possessively resting on the pony's reins. As soon as she appeared in the entryway, he frowned at her from where he stood by his horse.

"How could ye?" he asked, his face so full of hurt, it actually made Greer's heart wince.

"We canna all have an easy life, lad." She reached to ruffle his hair, but he pulled his head back.

His wounded gaze locked on hers. "How could ye take Brevis?"

She lifted a brow. "Brevis?"

"My horse." He gently stroked a hand down the pony's glossy brown neck. "He means so much to me and ye..." His jaw clenched, and he looked away, angry tears burning in his eyes.

A similar memory of Mac in such an agitated state wound its way into her awareness. "Forgive me," she said earnestly. "I dinna realize he means that much to ye."

"He does."

"Will ye tell me why?" she coaxed.

Lads Bean's age—probably only a summer or two older than Mac, but still so similar—liked to pretend they didn't need to share their thoughts, but like anyone else, they simply wanted to be heard and taken seriously.

Bean gazed up at her, the hurt narrowing in shrewdness. "Will ye tell me why ye stole from us?"

His request took her aback, but she nodded, knowing she couldn't be entirely honest with her reply.

"I picked him out myself five summers ago." Bean gave a little smile and rubbed his hand over the horse's velvety nose. "I could have any horse I wanted. Even a destrier like Drake. But I saw Brevis, and he was small. Like me. Small but fierce, as my da says," he amended with pride. He gave a sheepish shrug. "I've no' had many friends, but I've always had Brevis."

Greer drew in a deep breath, but it did nothing to assuage the pain of her culpability. "I dinna know he was so dear to ye."

"And ye? Why did ye do it?" he asked, brushing aside her remark as if he had never been wounded.

Bravado. So very like a lad around this age.

So very like Mac.

"Why did ye steal from us?" Bean asked again.

Before she could answer, the crunch of footsteps in the hard-packed dirt came from behind her and Drake's voice filled her silence. "I'd like to know as well."

She straightened and regarded Drake in his finery, his strong body well-fed. The unfairness of her lot in life came rushing back to her. It wasn't his fault he'd had it all so easy, but she could not stop her reaction from blazing in her cheeks.

I t was impossible for Drake not to notice the immediate change that fell over Greer when he joined her and Bean, his sword once more in place at his hip. Her shoulders stiffened, and her expression turned hard

"I was hungry," she replied simply.

"Ye had just eaten," Bean protested in an exasperated tone. "Master Fletcher fed ye a full meal at his own expense. We were only going to have a bit of bread and cheese near the stream and then have a full supper after we'd finish traveling for the day."

He opened his mouth to say more, but Drake shook his head to stop the lad. Bean closed his lips with chagrin.

"I dinna mean I was hungry now," Greer went on. "I mean, I've been hungry my whole life. Yer fine sword, yer well-bred horse—they would have brought me enough coin to eat for many months, mayhap a year. What I took, I thought ye could easily replace."

"Never." Bean stroked his horse.

Drake felt similarly about the sword at his side, its blade newly and needlessly sharpened. He had always been meticulous about his weapon, often gliding the whetstone over its length to ensure the edge was so fine, it could split a hair in half.

"Ye dinna know what it's like. To starve. To be cold. To no' always have a place to sleep." She angrily shook her head and strode away, her gait clipped with agitation.

"Wait," Bean called after her. "We want to help."

Drake put a hand up to stop the lad's paltry attempt. "Stay here with our horses." He didn't wait to see if Bean complied before chasing after Greer.

She hastened her pace as he closed in on her, clearly trying to get away swiftly.

"Greer," he called.

She ignored him.

He was near enough now to touch her, to let his hand skim over hers if he so desired but did not and instead called her name once more.

She spun about with flashing green eyes, her cheeks bright with her fury. "Leave me be," she said sharply.

He knew that facade, the one of anger and contempt, the one that was an easier emotion to embrace than what it hid. Hurt.

She had been caught trying to steal; she had been laid vulnerable for who she was in their eyes. And she didn't like it any more than they did. For as much as she was trying to be strong and defiant, he knew her to be broken.

"We want to help ye," he said softly.

"Because ye think I need charity." She scoffed. "I can fend well enough for myself."

"Aye," he said. "I know ye can. But we dinna want ye to."

"And ye mean to save me?" she asked bitterly.

Aye. But he didn't say that. Not when he knew she wouldn't take his reassurance the way it was meant. But he did wish he could save her, that he could soothe the wounds she had experienced in her life and that he could protect her from everything else.

"We mean to help ye home," he said instead.

She folded her arms over her chest. "Ye dinna think I can make it there on my own."

"I dinna doubt ye could make it there on yer own." He offered a gentle smile. "But I want to ensure ye have food as ye do. That ye can travel faster and have a place to sleep at night that is safe."

"Because I'm poor, and ye think I'm bonny." A strange expression moved over her face, almost a smirk. But before he could place it, it was gone.

He let his smile drop so she could discern the earnestness of his next words. "Because I too know what it is like to go without food, no' to know when I might have a place to sleep."

She stared at him for a long moment before giving a mirthless laugh and shaking her head. "Ye must think me a fool. No man offers anything and expects nothing in return."

"Ye have my word as a future knight that I will see ye to yer destination safely." He held out his hand.

Her dark lashes lowered as she regarded his upturned palm.

"We go as far as Lochmaben," he said.

Her gaze flicked up toward him with a flash of recognition.

"Do ye know of it?" he asked in surprise.

"I've heard of it."

"Are ye traveling near there? Ye said ye were going south." He was pressing too hard, he knew, and forced himself to stop talking.

A breeze swept past them and sent a tendril of her auburn hair trailing over her face. She brushed it away absently. "Near enough."

That would be all the answer he would get. Vague. Inspired by a lack of trust.

His sisters had him to protect them, but this woman undoubtedly had no one.

Something pulled in his chest, and he was hit with a sudden

need for her to join them, so he could at least offer her protection on the two-day journey to the English-Scottish border.

"We can take ye as far as Lochmaben and ensure ye have food and are protected on the journey." He smiled again to put her at ease. "As ye're well aware, ye'll get south faster with horses than on foot."

Her gaze narrowed again with skepticism. "Why are ye doing this?"

Drake glanced over his shoulder at Bean, who was stroking a brush over his horse's coat. "The lad likes ye. He was worried about ye."

A smile quirked the corner of her pretty mouth. "I thought he was angry with me."

"He was hurt." Drake lifted a brow. "Anger is easier than admitting as much."

Her stare slid away from his in quiet understanding at his words. After all, she too had fallen prey to the transference of emotions.

"Ye'll come then?" In truth, he shouldn't offer at all. He ought to walk away from her, leave her to her thieving.

Everything he had ever wanted was in Lochmaben. The king was counting on him.

Drake was a fool to want her to join them. And yet, he regarded her with a rare prickle of impatience, wishing she would accept his offer.

Greer's focus went past him to where Bean continued to brush his pony, and finally, she nodded. "Aye, I'll join ye."

The anxious tension drained from Drake's shoulders. At least while they traveled, he could help her. And after all, it was only two days. And how much of a distraction could she possibly cause on a two-day journey?

GREER HAD LEARNED LONG AGO NOT TO ACCEPT HELP. ALREADY a twist of unease drew tight in her lower stomach for going against everything she knew.

Except that Drake had appeared so earnest as he regarded her with his dark eyes, his square jaw set with determination. As if he truly did mean to save her.

The idea was laughable. No one ever meant to save her. Only to lead her into a trap.

She'd been fool enough to fall prey in her youth. But she was not some doe-eyed lass. Not anymore. Aye, she'd be going to bed that night with a dagger tucked under her pillow. It had saved her before, and it would doubtless save her again now.

She would have declined the ridiculous offer to accompany them. Except for Bean. Damn him, but the lad recalled thoughts of Mac so viscerally that she couldn't shake the endearing connection to him. Especially knowing that she had caused the lad hurt when she'd taken his pony.

It was true too—she would arrive in Lochmaben far quicker by horseback than by foot. And every day was precious.

Drake regarded her for a long moment, unspoken questions drawing his otherwise generous mouth into a line of tension. She didn't wait for them to emerge and instead made her way past him and toward Bean.

"I hope ye're no' too displeased with me." She reached out and ruffled Bean's thick hair. "I hope ye and Brevis can forgive me."

"So long as ye promise never to do it again." The lad raked his fingers through his hair to set it back in place.

"I'll be traveling with the two of ye," she added. "If ye dinna mind."

A flush crept over his cheeks, and he ducked his head to hide a broad grin. "I dinna mind."

His mood immediately elevated as he prepared Brevis for their departure with measured care that Greer had missed before. Now that she knew of his affection for the creature, it was incredibly evident by the gentle tone he used and the tenderness with which he held the reins.

"I should like to ride on until it grows dark." Drake helped her onto the saddle before swinging up behind her. "Then we'll find a place to rest."

Once more, he kept his body rigidly held away from her, his arms framed out to the sides to avoid brushing against her. They rode like that for some time until the sun began to descend in a wash of golden light that set the clouds aflame with reds, yellows and oranges amid the backdrop of a purple sky.

"If ye're tired, ye needn't worry," Bean said to her. "We'll be stopped soon. Aye?" He glanced to Drake, who must have nodded from behind Greer, for Bean shifted his focus back to the trail.

"And anyway, we willna be traveling for any real length of time," the lad continued. "'Tis only two days to Lochmaben. My da says travel is good for one's constitution."

"Why are ye going to Lochmaben?" Greer asked casually, knowing she was likely to get more from Bean than she would from Drake. For while Drake claimed to be honorable, she would remain suspicious until he'd proved otherwise. After all, he was not the first to make such a claim.

Drake shifted slightly behind her now as though uncomfortable with the question.

"We go to the castle there," Bean answered without hesitation. "The guards were so overwhelmed from the constant attacks; they've had to send fresh men down south to help defend the border should the English return to attack again. We're being sent to train the men, to make them proper warriors." At this, his chest puffed out. Indeed, even Brevis seemed to stand a mite taller with pride.

"Are ye as good as all that?" Greer asked with a smile, knowing it was Drake's skills being sought rather than that of the lad.

Still, it was Bean who answered. "One does what one can, my lady."

Drake remained silent.

If nothing else, at least the man wasn't a braggart.

But still, their reason for traveling to Lochmaben was all the more proof why she ought to keep her purpose to herself. If they were venturing to the castle to aid the guards, no doubt they held the same beliefs as those who had captured Mac.

Mayhap they might be able to help, but if they believed the earl over her—as they were surely wont to do—she would be taken prisoner along with her brother.

Nay, it was not worth the risk. Her affairs were best left unspoken.

The world around them had gone from the fiery notes of sunset to the darkening of dusk. The sun took longer to set in the summer, which meant Greer had been in the saddle for quite some time. Though she would prefer to pretend she did not feel any discomfort, she could not help but acknowledge the low ache in her back and grind of hunger at her stomach.

While she refused to say anything, she hoped they would stop soon. If nothing else, for a respite from the way she sat forward to avoid Drake, whose back surely must also be causing him pain.

No sooner had she thought these words than the thick forest of trees gave way to a clearing with a village at its center, seemingly out of nowhere.

"I dinna even see this in the distance." Greer looked back over her shoulder.

"When ye travel as often as I do, ye know what to look for," Drake replied.

He guided his horse to the village center and toward the nicer of the two inns available. Her stomach swirled with anxiety as they dismounted before the establishment. She knew what to expect.

No doubt Drake would return and swear there were only two rooms, one for Bean and one for her and Drake. He would offer to share the room but vow not to touch her. At least until they were alone, and the door was bolted shut.

She clenched her teeth, suddenly wishing to be back in the saddle, enduring the trail a little longer.

"Beathan, tend to the horses," Drake ordered.

The lad nodded and strode away with their steeds, his crooning voice drifting on the breeze as he spoke softly to them.

"Are ye coming?" Drake asked her.

Greer startled, sure he'd meant for her to wait outside while he secured the rooms. She nodded and followed him inside.

It was an inn like any other, spotted with people and barely lit by dull candlelight from tallow candles, their bases pooled with the melted fat whose odor permeated the thick air. A few people stopped and turned their way, some with interest as they fell on her. She ignored them, as she always did and shrank into herself, eager to disappear from their view.

A harried innkeeper with an armful of folded blankets regarded Drake with his brows lifted in obvious impatience. "What can I do for ye?"

"Three rooms, please," Drake said.

Ah, here it was. This was most likely someone Drake knew well, one he'd used this trick on often enough in the past that there need be no discussion beforehand on the façade of only two rooms being available.

"Three?" The innkeeper repeated, his brow furrowed as he appeared to be considering in his head.

Greer swallowed down the urge to dash from the stuffy inn.

The innkeeper indicated to the upper floor with a jerk of his head. "First three on the right. Will ye be supping as well?"

Greer blinked in surprise, but Drake did not notice as he nodded in response to the man's question.

"Una will aid ye." He lifted a pile of blankets a little higher. "I'm a bit taken at the moment."

Drake waved in understanding and led Greer to a table where

they sat opposite one another in companionable silence before Una, a slender woman with dark hair, approached the table for their order.

The very idea of food had lost its appeal to Greer. Aye, Drake was not trying to press his advance on her now, but no doubt once the candles were doused and they were abed, he would come rapping at her door.

It was only a matter of time.

❧ 6 ❧

As it turned out, Greer's appetite was not as diminished as she had assumed. She and Bean were expensive travel companions considering how much stew, bread and ale they consumed between the two of them.

They were just finishing their meal when Bean straightened. "Oy! That man took the coins the others left behind for Una."

Greer turned in her seat to find a man striding away from a previously occupied table, his hand conspicuously cupped as though he were cradling several coins against his palm.

Bean began to rise from the table, but Drake put a hand to his shoulder and pushed up to approach the man instead. The thief gave a contrite scowl at Drake's approach.

Whatever was said between them was impossible to hear, however through it all, Drake kept his calm demeanor. His straight, easy posture exuded an unspoken yet potent confidence Greer could not help being drawn toward. She had spent her life around people who either had no strength in themselves or had so much they couldn't stop bragging.

Suddenly, the other man's face went florid with rage as he gestured wildly with his free hand. It mattered not. The cool expression on Drake's face did not change. He remained taciturn and composed, even as the other man continued to grow more agitated, until at last the man stalked to the table still littered with empty cups and trenchers and slammed his hand upon the surface. Mugs jumped from the wobbly surface, one clattering to the floor, but when he lifted his hand, there on the table were three coins.

He stormed from the tavern, vowing never to return and Drake, nodding humbly at Una's profuse gratitude, returned to their table as if nothing had happened.

"That was brilliant," Bean exclaimed. "I thought he was going to clout ye. Though I dinna think he could handle a hit back. Ye'd have had him in one strike. Mayhap two."

"'Tis better to have been resolved as it was." Drake regarded their own nearly empty table. "Shall we retire? We leave again at first light."

The food stuffed into Greer's full belly suddenly was too great for the roil of nervousness trying to churn in the cramped space.

"Just one hit then," Bean continued as he got up and mimed the act of throwing his fist at the air. "It would have been amazing to see. I saw my da do it once, though he says the same as ye, that 'tis better to resolve with words." He grinned so broadly that the largeness of his front teeth was very apparent.

Greer rose slowly and followed behind them.

"Are ye well?" Drake's dark gaze fixed on her.

Mayhap she ought to say she was not in the hope he wouldn't try to come to her that night. But then, mayhap, he would leave her in the morning to travel the rest of the way on her own if he thought her ill.

She nodded and offered him a plastered smile she'd done enough times to know it passed off as being real.

"Imagine if there were three men," Bean said as he climbed the stairs. "Could ye have taken them then?" He nodded for Drake. "I know ye could."

His excited chatter filled the space and allowed Greer to slip away and into the first door on the right. Quickly, she slid the latch into place, a meager thing comprised of a leather thong and a wooden toggle, but better than nothing. She leaned her back against the door as another barrier and let her head rest against the solid wood.

This would be a long night indeed.

She remained there a long moment as Bean and Drake bid their brusque evening farewells before returning to their respective rooms. Silence filled the space, leaving only the whoosh of her heart pulsing in her ears. She counted each beat as she waited for the squeak of Drake's door opening to break the quiet.

To know he would be coming.

One, two. Three, four. Five, six.

Nothing.

Seven, eight. Nine, ten. Eleven, twelve.

When she reached one hundred, she eased away from the door, resolved to anticipate him most likely within the next hour. But she couldn't very well stand by the door all night. Not when her eyes were so weighted with exhaustion.

She kept her focus on the door as she hurried to the ewer to freshen up from her travel and prepare for bed. Normally, she would sleep in her shift.

Not tonight.

She left her kirtle on. While it would not be comfortable to lay in, it was an additional barrier of protection.

A slight creak came from outside her door.

Greer spun to face it; her dagger tucked behind her back, heart hammering. Her muscles were locked in preparation for a fight. One that never came.

The footsteps outside were attached to an unfamiliar male voice that carried down the hall moments later, along with his heavy tread.

Body tense, she finally backed toward the bed and sat on the edge.

Her limbs were heavy, like baskets of sodden laundry, and were suddenly scarcely strong enough to hold her upright. Still hesitant, she relaxed onto the lumpy mattress, setting the ropes beneath her groaning in protest.

She kept her face toward the door, the blanket over her like a flimsy shield, blade tucked beneath her pillow, ears trained for even the slightest sound, and willed sleep to come.

It did not, of course. Not when anticipation was such a sorry bedfellow.

The anxiety of waiting was worse than if the damn door had opened and Drake had entered, brazen with entitlement for what she would never let him have. Any moment now, no doubt.

Time ticked by, each second excruciating with expectation.

But no matter how much she begged sleep to find her, the poignant fear at the back of her mind continued to keep her alert. With a hiss of irritation, she shoved back the thin blanket and pushed upright.

She couldn't stand the waiting anymore. If she were to face this, she would do it on her own bloody terms.

Her feet met the cold floor as she shoved herself to standing and went out the door of her rented room, intent on seeing Drake.

๑๕๑

THE SOFT PATTER OF BARE FEET ON THE WOODEN FLOORS WAS what woke Drake from the depth of his slumber. He remained in place as a slight creak announced the person had opened his door.

Though his body tensed, he did not move.

His door wasn't locked. It was something he seldom did, not when there was so little point in bothering with it. Those flimsy toggles could be easily pushed through. It was better to allow a person to assume they had the advantage over him as he lay in wait to attack.

The door closed once more and the quiet whisper of footsteps moved over the floor to his bed. Whatever they were planning to do to him, he would make his move first.

Quick as a serpent's strike, he grabbed the intruder and threw them to the bed.

A soft gasp sucked in as he trapped the person on the bed by their arms. Slender arms. Arms that would not properly be able to wield a sword to slay him in his sleep.

His gaze went to the face, the dark lashes and the auburn arch of a brow highlighted in a slash of moonlight that still hid most of her face. Not that he needed to see more to know her.

Greer.

He released her immediately. She didn't scramble away from him, but stayed where she lay beneath him, breasts heaving.

"What are ye doing here?" he demanded.

"I know what ye want," she accused.

He frowned at her. "A solid night's sleep before the journey tomorrow?"

"I'll no' lay with ye," she said vehemently. A flush of red crept over her cheeks in the pale light.

He put more space between them. "I dinna intend to lay with ye."

She blinked up at him. He rose from the bed and lifted his hands to demonstrate his innocence.

"I'm no' daft." She sat up, and the dress pulled up higher over her legs, revealing her shapely calves. She whipped the length of fabric back down. "I know how this works."

"Then I think I must be the daft one," he said slowly. "Because I dinna understand what ye're going on about."

She slid from the bed and stared first at his naked torso, then slowly lifted her gaze to meet his eyes. Her head only came to his chest, reminding him of exactly how petite she was.

"I know why ye paid for my meal, why ye let me share yer horse," she said with an edge to her voice.

"Because we want to help ye," he said. "As we discussed in the village today."

She scoffed, a hard, bitter sound. "Ye think I've no' heard that before?"

He regarded her face fully now, taking in the rage burning bright in her eyes. And the underlying fear beneath. "What has been done to ye, Greer?" he asked softly.

The anger flickered to uncertainty. "What do ye mean?"

Her skin looked impossibly smooth in the moonlight. He lifted his hand slowly and settled his palm against her soft, warm cheek. She gazed up at him, her eyes wide with innocence or hurt, or mayhap a blend of both. Either way, her expression snagged a place in his heart where it would forever stay.

"What has been done to ye?" he asked again softly.

Her lashes fluttered closed at the tender caress, and a tear ran down her cheek. She swallowed but did not reply.

"Whatever has been done willna happen again while ye are in my care," he said with all the earnestness he could summon in his soul. "Ye need no' worry about anything while we are traveling together. No one will hurt ye."

Her eyes flew open, and her chin quivered. He lowered his hand to ensure she didn't see him as a threat. But he didn't want to. He wanted to draw her closer to him, in a complete embrace where he would shield her entire body in the protection of his, so that he might be able to insulate her from any threat.

Before he could say anything further, she turned on her heel and bolted from the room. He remained where he stood for a long time, a band of tension squeezing in his chest.

She viewed him as much of a danger as she had all the men who had harmed her in the past.

A part of him longed to go to her room, to reassure her he was not like the others. Yet he knew doing so would only leave her to fear that he was exactly like them, prepared to exact a steep fee for his aid.

Revulsion coiled in his gut for such men.

He turned away from the door at last and settled in his bed. Though she had only lain on the mattress for a short moment, the sweet smell of her lingered on the sheets, the scent subtle and clean. It brought to his mind the image of her laid out, staring up at him, cheeks flushed and eyes flashing.

With a violent shove of his thoughts, he cast the image from his mind. Aye, she was bonny. Aye, everything about her tempted him in a way he'd never known. But he would rather cut a limb from his body than give way to any of those impulses. Especially with what she'd been through.

He had more control than that.

But despite his determination, thoughts of her remained with him all night until the sun finally spilled its golden light into his room, and he was left weighted by a heavy veil of exhaustion to prepare for the journey.

Bean was waiting at a table downstairs a while later with a scowl on his face.

"I take it ye dinna sleep well either?" Drake asked.

"'Tis hard when one who should be above reproach canna mind themself." He glared at a pockmark on the table.

Drake swallowed down a weary sigh and sank onto the bench opposite him. Whatever it was that rankled Bean would be best addressed before Greer joined them. "What troubles ye, lad?"

Bean shifted his glare up at Drake. "I saw her entering yer room last night." A flush warmed over his cheeks. "She went to see ye."

"And if ye'd waited a bit longer, ye'd have seen her leave soon after," Drake replied.

Bean folded his arms over his thin chest. "What did she want?"

Una arrived then with several ales and bowls of pottage. Drake accepted them from her and gratefully drank.

"Wrong room," he lied as he set the mug on the table. While he didn't relish offering mistruths to the lad, neither did he wish to embarrass Greer.

She came down the stairs at that very moment with shadows under her eyes that were indicative of her own night of troubled rest.

"How did ye end up in the wrong room last night?" Bean demanded.

"All the doors look the same." She laughed it off and reached over him for a slice of bread, which she set into her bowl of pottage as she plunked onto the bench beside him.

"Then why did ye stay at all when ye realized it wasna the right room?" the lad pressed.

"'Twas dark and took me a moment to realize," she answered with ease. "And then I begged forgiveness for having interrupted Drake's slumber."

The mirth on her face was as false as the words falling from her lips, but Bean, in his innocent youth, appeared placated. Yet while the lad ate with the zeal of adolescence, Drake could not stop the queries from rising in his mind.

There was much more to Greer than the façade she offered the world, and he wanted to know exactly who she was.

Agreeing to travel with the two of them had been a mistake. Greer realized that now. Drake was no ordinary man. He saw her more deeply than anyone else. Beyond the layers that she'd built like calluses over the years, past the prettiness most men allowed themselves to be distracted by and straight into the sloughed away rawness of her heart.

She'd expected he would be a man who would try to work an advantage over her, as most did. To her dismay, he was far, far worse. His unassuming nature edged past her defenses, and some-how, he managed to see who she was inside. He could identify the emotions she tried to hide from—the fear and the wounded hurt —and offered her something she knew she should never again bother with. Hope.

Once, long ago, she had held hope, as if a flickering flame in the cradle of her soul. Back when Mac had first been born. Before her mother had left and her father lost himself in the bottle. When days had been sunny, and their food stores had been sufficient.

But when she had to start stealing to feed them, it had slipped away, as if a cloud passed over the sun, blotting its warmth and light.

Foolishly, she had dared to hope again when she bought the tiny cottage with her earnings from laundering clothes in the village. A hard living to be sure, but an honest one. That life had brought her happiness and hard-won pride.

But that bliss had been precarious, balanced on the whims of their unjust lord who captured Mac, leaving them at the mercy of laws that did not favor the poor. In an instant, that joy had been snuffed out. And with it, her hope.

She was not so foolish as to let it be reignited so easily.

"Have ye had enough?" Drake indicated her half-eaten pottage, which was growing cold where it congealed against the side of the wooden bowl.

She'd avoided glancing at him thus far but now forced herself to as she nodded. No sooner had her gaze settled on his dark eyes than the memories from the previous night flooded her mind.

The way he had touched her cheek so gently, not with ownership or intent, but with affection. Compassion. A band of emotion compressed around her.

He had promised to protect her. She looked away suddenly as a prickle of tears warmed in her eyes. No one had protected her for as long as she could remember. *She* had protected her. No one else.

While she could not even fathom what such a thing must feel like, there was a part of her that yearned with palpable longing to find out.

And if ever there was someone capable of such a thing, it would be a man like him—one whose body was etched with muscle. Not noticing such had been impossible when she'd been in his room. He'd worn only a pair of linen trews, his torso stripped bare and carved like granite in the moonlight.

She had never found herself interested in intimacy, not when so many men had been readily drawn to her. But seeing Drake thus had made her curious for the sensation of his naked skin beneath her palms, for the slight rasp beneath her fingernails as she traced the lines of muscle.

A strange feeling tightened in her stomach and heated her blood. One she did not welcome or recognize.

She kept her focus on the floor as they rose from the table, as though the dark stains in the grooves of wood from years of ground-in dirt were overly fascinating. They had only two more days and one more night before they would arrive in Lochmaben.

Mac.

He was her sole concern. Him, and acquiring enough coin to ensure his freedom.

The day before, she'd thought her task accomplished with what she had stolen from Drake and Bean, only to have it all taken away. She was once more back where she started with not much more than a couple of coins jingling in her otherwise empty purse.

The sun had risen by the time they departed the tavern. The light of a new day was brilliant in the clear sky as they resumed their journey. Only this time, Greer found herself wishing Drake's hands weren't as far from her as they had previously been when she rode with him. She wondered at the heat of those strong arms enfolded around her, offering the protection he had promised.

As they rode, she did not keep herself as stiff as she had before. Instead, she relaxed in the saddle, so her bottom grazed his crotch. Immediately, he jerked back and readjusted his position, so no part of his body connected with her.

It only made her want to touch him more, but she did not wish to force him so far back that he fell from the horse. She resolved to stifle her interest and remain still in the saddle. At least, until the previous night's sleeplessness overtook her, and exhaustion tugged at her lids.

The thick foliage overhead provided coolness from the direct glare of the sun, dappling their path with flecks of gilded light.

The damp scent of rich soil and wet leaves from the woods rose around her, clean and welcoming. Were it not for the sway of the horse, she might have been fine.

Her head nodded first, bowing over her chest before falling backward. She snapped awake, only to repeat the awkward gesture.

Suddenly, the strong wall of Drake's torso was there.

"Ye can rest against me to sleep." His voice was gentle and low in her ear.

A shiver of chills tickled over her skin. But nothing like the revulsion that assaulted her with other men. Nay, this was far warmer and certainly welcome.

Sensual.

But he mistook the shiver for something else and stiffened. "I willna take advantage of ye, Greer," he said vehemently. "I meant what I said last night, lass." His voice was a whisper to keep Bean from hearing, and it was like velvet against her ear. "I'll no' let anyone hurt ye."

She nodded in acknowledgment and relaxed back against Drake's strong chest, letting her head rest to the side. He was warm and solid, with his light scent of leather and horse and a spicy, unfamiliar yet entirely pleasant smell that made the place between her thighs begin to pulse.

Her nostrils flared slightly as she breathed him in, reveling in his heat and power. She recalled how he had promised to protect her, and a strange sensation loosened in her chest.

Safe.

For the first time in her life, she felt safe.

His heartbeat thudded against her cheek where she lay her head. It was to that rhythmic beat that she finally found herself drifting off to sleep.

She didn't know how long she remained thus, but her awareness roused when the horse's steady swaying came to a stop.

"Greer," his voice was scarcely a whisper in her ear as if he worried that he might frighten her.

Only then did the bustle of people and chatter of voices fill her awareness. She blinked her eyes open to find they were on the outskirts of a village. But it was not yet night.

"What are we doing?" she asked, her mind still addled with exhaustion.

"We need provisions," Drake said. "I thought ye'd prefer to wake before we went into the village."

Heat flooded Greer's cheeks, and she sat upright. "Aye, thank ye." She frowned. "I thought we had provisions. The meat and cheese from this morn."

Drake cleared his throat. "They were consumed."

Bean shrank into his shoulder guiltily as his cheeks flushed. "I was still hungry," he offered by way of scant apology.

She couldn't help but chuckle at that. Mac was always the same way, eating whatever he could lay his hands on, oftentimes even when it was meant to be supper.

"'Tis the way with lads," she offered in sympathy, which earned her a grateful smile from the adolescent.

In truth, she did not mind the diversion. It would offer her an opportunity to pilfer a few items. While she would be arriving in Lochmaben sooner, her purse would still be near empty and lacking the bribe needed to free her brother.

Drake leapt from his horse, and she accepted his help down, unable to keep from noticing how he handled her as though she were something fragile that might break.

Together they led the horses into the village, where the press of people at its center indicated market day was in full swing. How fortuitous!

Pockets were heavier on market day, and larger crowds were the perfect shield for her clandestine acts.

She brushed past a man in a leather jerkin and slid the purse from his side. It was not weighty enough for its absence to be noted but still had several coins within. It passed easily into her bag. She scanned the square to confirm no one had seen her.

She wandered toward a woman wearing an elegant silk gown, the hem dusty from where it carelessly dragged in the dirt. A sweep past her with a steady hand loosened the thin gold chain that had been clasped around the woman's kirtle. It fell into Greer's palm, the metal cold against the heat of her skin.

Except she was not as lucky as before and her action did not go unnoticed. Nay—this time, she had been snared by Bean's pointed gaze.

"She's stealing again," Bean hissed.

"How do ye know?" Drake turned to where Greer glanced nonchalantly away from them and wandered toward a small stand of pastries shimmering with a coat of honey over their flaky crusts.

"I saw her." Bean didn't take his eyes from her as he spoke. "She slipped the woman's gold belt off."

The woman he referenced continued to walk about the market, inspecting a bolt of fabric with a slight scowl before moving onto a merchant selling ribbons in myriad colorful streamers that danced in the breeze. She appeared unaware of her lost item.

The trip into the village was supposed to be a swift one, most especially not one steeped in thievery. Drake didn't bother to hide his wariness as Greer approached them with two pastries in her hand.

"Did ye steal those?" Bean asked.

Her mouth fell open in offense. "Of course no', but I did get ye one." She handed a pastry to Bean.

The sweet, honeyed scent of the treat wafted up toward

Drake. Surely the lad was tempted, yet Bean still didn't accept it and instead turned away. "I'll no' eat something stolen."

"I dinna steal it." She turned and waved to the man who sold the pastries. He held up a hand back, his face set in a wide grin.

That was enough to convince Bean, who plucked the treasure from her hand. He paused only to murmur a quick thanks before sinking his teeth into the flaky sweet.

Greer's green eyes boldly met Drake's. "I'll split mine with ye." She set her fingers at the back while holding the sides with her thumb in preparation for halving it.

Drake shook his head. "Nay, ye bought it. Keep it for yerself but thank ye."

"I dinna buy it."

Bean stopped chewing, and his eyes went wide.

She laughed. "He gave them to me."

"Why?" Bean asked.

"Because I asked." She shrugged and took a bite.

"Because ye asked?" Drake narrowed his eyes, not understanding. "Did the lady also offer for ye to take her belt?"

Greer bit into her pastry again, as if she hadn't heard him.

"Beathan, see to the horses," Drake ordered, preferring the lad not to be around when having the necessary conversation with Greer.

Fortunately, Bean offered no protest as he returned to the horses, pastry in hand, still constrained to his role as the squire, even if Drake was not a knight. Yet.

"Ye asked, and he gave them to ye?" Drake pressed.

Greer tilted her head with exasperation. "I told him it was Bean's natal day today, and I wanted a treat for him, but dinna have my purse on me. He offered me two."

"So ye lied." An ache was settling in Drake's head, one he tried to ward off by pinching the bridge of his nose.

"Nay." Greer blocked the sun with the flat of her hand as her mouth slid up into a crafty smile. "I dinna know when the actual date of his birth is. Indeed, it might have been today so far as I knew."

"And the woman's chain?" He tempered the rise of his anger. If it were known that he traveled with a thief, she could jeopardize his opportunity to become a knight. If she were caught and found in his care...

Greer pursed her lips. "Aye, I stole that." She dropped her hand so the full light of the sun highlighted her brilliant eyes. "I'm assuming ye want me to return it."

Drake gritted his back teeth, and Greer sighed. "Verra well." She reached into her bag and withdrew a golden chain. It glinted against her raw palm, the fineness of the jewelry making the calluses and cracks of her worn hands all the more apparent.

With a resigned look up at him, she disappeared, blending into the crowd somehow.

Nay, not somehow—strategically. That much was evident in the way she hunched a little lower, ducked her head and rolled her shoulders forward. She was clever, he would give her that. But while she was skilled at thieving, she evidently did not shy from hard work, as was obvious by her hands.

But why had she stopped her hard work and resorted to stealing? What happened to bring her to Dunfermline?

In the distance, she approached the woman and offered a shy bow that appeared genuinely reticent. Drake couldn't help but smirk. Greer was never reticent. But the woman did not appear put off. Rather, her face lit up in surprise as her hands went to her waist. She took the chain from Greer with a grateful incline of her head as her servant handed a coin to Greer, who readily pocketed the money.

Once the exchange was done, she strode back to him and tossed him a displeased look.

"Ye dinna tell her ye took it," he surmised.

"At least I returned it," she replied.

"And received payment for its return."

She simply smiled at him.

"Greer," he said in a quieter voice. "Ye canna steal while we're traveling together."

"We canna all afford to be as high and mighty as ye," she shot back.

He pressed his lips together. She would never understand what he'd been through, not when she couldn't see past his fine clothes and heavy purse. "Ye dinna have to steal."

Her gaze drifted toward the market, distancing herself from their conversation. "Ye dinna know anything about my life."

"I'd like to," he answered earnestly. "I'd like to help, so ye dinna need to fall back on a life of thievery."

"Ye want to help," she repeated in a flat tone. "Fifty marks would do."

He lifted his brows at the ridiculous sum. "Aye, I'm sure it would."

Her mouth curled into a pretty smile. "There ye are, then." With that, she strode back toward the horses, her shoulders still hunched forward. Though this time, he suspected it had little to do with blending in and more with the torrent of emotion behind her shielded expression.

She hesitated a moment in her path. Only then did he see a small child sitting against a wall of the alleyway, his palm upturned. Greer pulled the coin she had received from her pocket and placed it in his hand.

Drake knew exactly how precious that coin was to her and what a sacrifice it was for her to give it up.

The act was generous and one of the many reasons why Drake fought so hard to protect her. She was a good woman at her core. Surely, there were circumstances at work to make her do as she did.

And he would find out what they were.

He had hoped that her anger might cool in the time that he obtained provisions for a substantial lunch, but the flush to her cheeks when he returned indicated it had not. When they climbed onto the horse together, she did not lean back as she had before but remained stiffly in front of him.

He had liked that she had trusted him enough earlier in the day to have slept against him. And though he'd tried not to watch her, nor admit it to himself, she was bonny as she slumbered. She'd had her head resting on his chest, her auburn hair coming loose from its braid to whisper softly against her flushed cheeks. Any defenses she had up were lowered, her face relaxed with ease.

That fragile trust had no doubt been broken by their exchange and was something he needed to address when they were alone. To explain not only his ire but his life so that she would understand. And to learn why she stole in the first place, for he suspected there was a reason for her deeds, and he had to know.

❦ 8 ❦

Frustration knotted through Greer as they traveled in silence. Drake and Bean would be watching her wherever they went. Making sure she didn't steal. Making sure she was living an honest life.

Ironically, that was all she'd ever wanted—an honest life.

Emotion welled in the back of her throat. She'd had that kind of existence and loved it. Before the wealthy noble took Mac and threw away her years of hard work.

If she couldn't steal while she traveled, she'd have to do it near Lochmaben and in the surrounding villages. She was no fool—she knew how dangerous it would be to lift so many purses in such proximity. After only a couple of days, all the villagers would be on the lookout for her.

And if she were caught...

Nay, she wouldn't think of that. She couldn't. Not with the price so high.

She clenched her fist with the determination to rescue Mac, no matter what it took.

They did not stop to rest that afternoon and instead ate as they traveled, but whatever conversation had blossomed between them the day prior fell away into nothing. Tension hummed in the air, and Greer had been the cause.

Guilt caught at her, followed immediately by the grip of helplessness at her predicament.

The makings of a solution did not come to her until they were at the inn. The establishment was of finer quality than the one the night before, its slate roof absent of white-streaked stains and its tavern area spread with fresh rushes that tempered the oily odor of tallow candles. They had few rooms to spare, and though Drake had been able to procure three for their group, they would not be near one another.

Suddenly a possibility blossomed in Greer's thoughts.

She could leave.

They had journeyed quite a distance already. The trip to Lochmaben would be considerably reduced by how far they'd traveled by horseback. It would give her the opportunity to pilfer the amount she needed while traveling.

But the idea did not bring her the relief she had hoped. Especially when she sat across from Drake and his dark eyes settled on hers. There was something in them she couldn't read, something that made a place in her chest grow warm.

After a few minutes passed without being approached for food and ale, Bean darted off to track down the barmaid, leaving her alone with Drake for a short moment. It was then he finally spoke for the first time since he'd caught her stealing in the village. "Greer, I—"

Bean came rushing back and plopped down on the bench with the pent-up energy of a boy who hadn't been able to run about all day. While Greer was left exhausted from the ride, no doubt Bean was grateful for a chance to stretch his long, skinny legs.

"She's coming," the lad said with a wide grin. "The innkeeper needed help with some blankets." He abruptly cut off and looked between them, his eyes narrowed with suspicion, but he didn't say anything more.

The ache was back in Greer's chest. She might never see Bean again after departing tonight. Or Drake.

She could recall too vividly how comfortable Drake's body had been while he cradled her to sleep on the horse. And how the moonlight had caressed his naked torso, unveiling his sculpted muscle in shadowed, sensual detail. Her cheeks blazed hot and she turned her attention to the bag at her side rather than allow Drake to see her flushed face.

Not that she ought to allow her attention to stray for even an instant. She still had the man's purse neither Bean nor Drake had seen her lift. Which meant she hadn't been forced to return it. While she hadn't had an opportunity to count out the coins, she guessed there were at least half a dozen, given the way the metal knocked about one another when she'd discreetly shaken it.

Mayhap there would be more.

"Is something amiss?" Bean asked.

"Nay," Greer and Drake said at the same time.

She frowned to herself. She knew why she was suddenly acting strangely, but why was Drake?

Bean's eyes narrowed further still, his skepticism evident. "What is—"

Before he could finish the question, the barmaid showed up with a platter of food, and his mouth was too busy for inquiries. But Greer had not forgotten and continued to observe Drake through the meal. Aye, he was indeed watching her, his expression unreadable.

As full of energy as Bean had been at the start of the meal, he was practically falling asleep where he sat after he'd eaten his fill, which made encouraging him up the flight of stairs to their rooms an easy task. Drake led the way, as sure and confident as always. Greer hesitated outside her door as Drake showed the lad to his room, hoping he would turn back to her and finish what it was he had to say.

He did exactly that and her heart galloped with a frenzy of anticipation.

His lips parted as if he wished to speak as he studied her. Something twisted inside her and told her she wouldn't like what he had to say. Was it another lecture on morality? Surely, it wasn't a proposition that would make him like every other man who had offered to help her. But what if it was? Or mayhap it was something that alluded to the sadness lingering in his gaze, something that would make abandoning him impossible.

"Rest well," she quickly said before he could fill the quiet between them with words she could not stand to hear.

He nodded once. "And ye."

She clutched her bag tight to her chest and pushed through her door. She unplaited her hair and pulled off her shoes as she waited for his heavy footsteps strode away. When the sound of his departure dissipated, she tugged her bag open and dug out the small purse she'd taken. It was newer, the leather still stiff as she loosened its laces and dumped the contents into her hand. Only five coins glinted dully up at her.

It was better than nothing, but such a bounty would be needed dozens of times over to equal the fifty marks she required. Disappointment left her limbs heavy, and her hands sagged into her lap. There was nothing for it—she would have to depart the following morning before Drake and Bean woke. To venture out on her own so she could steal enough funds to afford her brother's freedom.

A knock sounded at the door, so unexpected that she nearly dropped the precious coins. She curled her hand into a fist and silently returned the money back into the purse and then into her bag before cautiously standing. "Who is it?"

When no one answered, she crept closer, her skin prickling with the awareness of exactly who it might be.

Drake.

There shouldn't be an attraction to such a consideration, but she could not quell the flip of her stomach at the very idea. If he were coming to her in the evening, it could doubtless be for only one purpose. It was not as unappealing as she had once thought. Indeed, an intoxicating warmth spreading in her veins said it was rather the opposite.

And if he could be encouraged to procure the fifty marks, well, better the devil she knew...

DRAKE DIDN'T KNOCK A SECOND TIME. HE SHOULDN'T HAVE knocked at all. Going to Greer's room was a poor decision, as his gut had told him from the first, but he'd foolishly ignored that.

This lass didn't need some man approaching her, especially not in the middle of the night. But how could he speak candidly with Bean nearby?

The lad would no doubt be listening to the entire conversation and offer commentary throughout. As if the right words would not already be hard enough to muster up without the overly righteous squire within earshot.

Aye, Drake ought to go, return to his chambers before someone saw him. Heaven help him if Bean happened to catch sight of him before Greer's bedchamber.

He stepped back, fully prepared to leave, when the door swung open. Greer stood there with her hair unbound from its usual braid, the rich auburn tresses falling in silky waves that scented the air with something floral he couldn't name but found he liked far more than he should.

"Forgive me," he said.

One auburn brow lifted. "For being here?" Bemusement played over her lips, an action that appeared to be intentionally sensual. She opened the door wider in silent invitation.

He stiffened at the impropriety. "I can speak from where I am."

She glanced about and furrowed her brows. "Where everyone can see ye? Mayhap just come in while no one is about, aye?"

Apparently, there was no good way to go about a private conversation without compromising her, so he swiftly stepped into her room. She closed the door behind him, locking him alone with her in the small space. The familiar sweet scent of her was everywhere in an intimate way he could not help but acknowledge.

He swallowed, and he turned to her. Her feet were bare below the frayed hem of her homespun dress. They were as slender and fair as the rest of her. Seeing her thus, so casual and at ease, felt like a glimpse into her private life, one he had no right to view. Suddenly the discomfort of intruding on her intensified. He truly should not have come.

"I..." He pulled his eyes from her feet and met her gaze. "Forgive me for my anger with ye earlier today."

"I stole. Ye're honorable." She shrugged as if that was all the explanation needed. "Is that why ye're here?"

It was, and it wasn't. He needed to explain to her how he had once lived so that she wouldn't feel judged. So she would understand. While the words had come easily enough as he thought them before, they were difficult to force aloud.

The way he had lived was never something he talked about, it was just something he had done. Survival. Struggle. One day at a time.

She stepped toward him and ran a hand through her hair, sweeping it back to reveal her bonny face in the firelight. And she was indeed bonny. Wide eyes fringed with dark lashes, a lush mouth, a pert nose sprinkled with freckles as perfectly as God had distributed stars among the night sky.

"I understand," Drake said abruptly. "Why ye steal."

She gave a mirthless laugh. "So ye keep saying."

"I wasna always so honorable," he admitted.

"A wealthy knight's son with too much time?" she surmised.

He frowned with distaste. "Nay."

She tilted her head in silent question.

"I was..." A knot of tension tightened at the back of his neck. "For years, I was a reiver."

The word was like ash in his mouth, the byproduct of his razed youth and the sacrifices he'd been forced to make. For reivers were thieves. They resided on the border between England and Scotland, their lot in life cast so poorly, they had only the prospect of stealing to keep food in the bellies of their families.

Reivers were men without honor.

Greer laughed again and shook her head. "Ye expect me to believe that?"

"Aye, because it's true." He ran his hands through his hair, wishing he had something to do with his hands, to take his focus from what he was about to tell her.

"But yer da was a knight," she protested.

"An English knight." He strode over to the fire and crouched to put another log into the flames, though it wasn't at all necessary to do so. "He was killed in a fight against the Scottish."

"But yer Scottish."

"Aye, on my mum's side. When he died, she had no one to help with my sisters and me. My da's liege lord gave me a sack of coins to compensate for his death, but it doesna last long when there are accounts to settle and when there are so many mouths to feed. Especially with people we'd once assumed to be friends being suddenly hostile." He watched the flames lick greedily over the tinder, curling and crackling at errant bits of splintered wood. "We had no choice but to travel back to Scotland."

"Ye're really being honest, aye?" Greer's voice drew his attention from the burning log.

He straightened from where he knelt by the hearth. "Aye. English friends turned spiteful when we had little ties to England after my da's death. They no longer saw us as any part English but as their enemy instead. There were many days we went without food, back when I was too young to make more money to feed us all."

Greer chewed her bottom lip as she watched him, her expression hesitant as if she were afraid to believe him.

"Ye say I dinna know hunger," he said. "But I can still recall the sharpness of it gnawing at my stomach. The way ye look at the grass and wonder if eating it might somehow stop that awful pain. I knew nights on the open road where we had no' the coin for an inn—when I couldna sleep for fear something might happen to my mum or my sisters. I lay awake, flinching at every sound, holding this verra sword." He set his palm on the sword at his hip. "Ye see me in my finery, but it wasna always this way. What ye dinna see are the years where we barely survived, when I went without so my sisters and mum could be fed and clothed and safe."

"I dinna know." Greer went to him, her bare feet silent on the scuffed wood floor. She reached for his hand.

Her caress was light, tender, and it soothed a ragged place inside him he hadn't known could be reached. Those lovely green eyes searched his gaze now, seeming to see down into his very soul. But he didn't look away as he might ordinarily do. Let her see him—let her realize why he rose above a life of thievery now, and see every horrible, hateful struggle he had lived through.

Let her see that he understood.

"I never speak of such things," he admitted.

Greer ran a finger over his jaw, the caress feather-light. "Ye've no' ever told anyone before?"

"Nay." He gently withdrew her hand from his face lest the temptation to touch her in return got the best of him. "My da was the most honorable man I've ever known," he continued. "I've always done what I could to be worthy of being his son. Having to resort to thievery to survive cost a piece of me I willna ever be able to get back."

She stared up at him, her eyes wide with an appreciation for what they shared.

He should back away, put space between them. Except that their closeness, and the way she saw him so completely, held him rooted in place. His hand rose and lightly brushed the edge of her jawline. Her skin was warm against his fingertips and made him crave to brush the rest of his fingers over her cheek.

"I dinna want that for ye," he whispered. "I want to protect ye."

She gave a gentle exhale that teased against his chin as tears sparkled in her eyes.

9

I want to protect ye.

It wasn't the first time he'd said as much, and the impact of those words was as visceral to Greer this time as they had been before. It loosened in her a poignant longing to allow herself to soften into his strong arms and let him envelop her in everything safe, so nothing bad could ever touch her again.

Heat tingled in her eyes, and she knew her emotions were overwhelming her. She swallowed. "'Tis too late for all that."

His brows flinched together, his expression pained.

"I'm already a consummate thief." The admission was not given boastfully. Indeed, she was not proud of her skill.

"Ye havena always stolen." He lowered his hand from her face and reached for her fingers, where the skin was still chapped from so many years of working with harsh lye soap. She understood what he was implying, but it changed nothing.

"Laundering doesna pay as well as stealing." She looked away, hating that such an honorable man would see her misdeeds laid so bare. "'Tis hard for a woman to make good money without a man."

He nodded. "I've always had my skill with a sword, I know.

But I watched my mother struggle for years to do whatever she could to provide us with food."

Greer pulled in a hard breath. Never before had she talked about her life with anyone. Not even Mac. What was the point when he was living it alongside her? Especially if he might feel guilty for what she did to ensure he had a meal in his stomach.

But then, Drake had shared his story with her, the hurt of their neighbors' betrayal in England plain on his face, the memories difficult to spill free from whatever dark place he had locked them in all those years ago. She had a similar place inside of herself, a place no one had ever cared to see opened before.

But then, no one had sought to protect her before, either.

Until now.

"My mum left when—" She stopped herself just in time to keep from saying their mother had left when Mac was two. If she mentioned Mac, Drake would want to know more about him, including where he was now.

It was then she reminded herself that Drake and Bean traveled to Lochmaben to secure the castle, the very place her brother was being held prisoner.

"My mum left when I was ten." She looked up at Drake to find him watching her intently, his large, blunt fingers still wrapped loosely around hers. There was a quiet comfort to the way he held her, offering consolation without expectation, and she found she rather liked it. "My da dinna care for anything, save the drink that left his throat on fire and his temper fierce. Were it no' for stealing, I'd have starved long ago."

It was such a simple explanation of all those terrible years—of trying to protect Mac from her da's staggering belligerence when the old drunk insisted that she must surely have money he could use for more whisky. It didn't detail the times she and Mac had fled the house to be safe from him or how they had found refuge in the streets. Greer understood too well Drake's inability to sleep in the open for fear of not being awake to keep his mother and sisters safe, for she had also experienced many a night when she hadn't slept to ensure her brother remained safe.

But she couldn't share as much, not when she was not yet comfortable mentioning Mac.

Drake's hand tightened more firmly around hers. Like a shield.

Greer felt her walls crumble but held them intact at the last minute. She could not tell this man, who meant to heighten the skill of Lochmaben Castle guards, that her brother was a prisoner within and she was gathering coin for a guard to be bribed. Nay, not when it might cost her Mac's life.

"No one has ever tried to protect me before," she admitted, a slight catch to her voice.

"But people have hurt ye," he surmised.

The emotion returned, clenching at the back of her throat in a hard, unyielding knot. She nodded, not trusting herself to speak at that moment.

A muscle worked in Drake's jaw as if he were reigning in his rage. Not at her. But at the men who had tried to hurt her.

"I dinna trust ye before..." She paused to clear her throat. "I dinna think I've ever received anything without having someone expect a favor for their efforts. Most men, they will expect a bonny lass to offer her appreciation. Especially wealthy men who assume because I am poor, I can be bought."

The muscle in his jaw ticked again. "Ye dinna have to—"

She shook her head to stop him. "I have never shared my story with anyone either."

He didn't protest again but folded his other hand on top of hers, sealing her gently in his large grip.

There, in the safety of that embrace, she finally spoke. "The first man who offered a place for me to stay forced himself into the room with me." She omitted how Mac had been with her, only five then and asleep so deeply, he hadn't roused. "I had a dagger with me." As was necessary when living on the streets. "I was able to fend him off, thanks be to God. It's been with me ever since and has helped me fend off many others." She patted the sheath at her belt where the knife resided when it was not tucked under her pillow.

"No one has ever offered to protect me before," she reiterated. There was that ache of anguish at the back of her throat again. She swallowed it away. "Not once in my entire life."

"I will keep ye safe," he vowed. "And if ye dinna trust me—"

She shook her head, not wanting him even to say those words, to make it apparent in the quiet room that while she trusted him more than she did any other man, she might never entirely trust him. Even her admission had the glaring absence of Mac. If she had trusted Drake completely, she would have told him about Mac. Mayhap asked for his aid.

But she trusted him more than she had anyone else. And for her, right now, that was enough.

It was more than enough. It made her body go warm, and her head spun with a lightness that drew her toward him. She wanted his strong body around her the way his hands had been, curling her in a shell of strength, a promise she wanted him to make good on.

She withdrew her hand from his and put it to his chest, where the thud of his heartbeat patted against her fingertips.

Drake glanced down at her hand, then lifted his gaze to regard her, his expression tender.

"Drake," she said in a quiet voice.

His nostrils flared. But he did not touch her. Nay, his arms remained at his side.

She wanted them to wrap around her, to secure her to him. Her focus went to his mouth. His lips were thinned with a determination she could practically feel emanating off him. A sudden longing to kiss them into submission overtook her.

She flattened her hand to his chest, so her palm caressed the place over his heart as she rose higher to bring her mouth within a breath of his. His heartbeat was no longer steady but wild and erratic.

Because of her.

The thought thrilled her. Usually, such a realization with other men left her filled with disgust. But not Drake. Nay, he made her blood go as hot as fire and her mind swarm with sin.

He was good. Moral. Handsome. A protector intent on saving her. And somehow, his asking for nothing in return made her want to give him everything.

"Greer," he said gently.

They were close enough that she could detect the slight spice of his breath, and it made her throb with desperation. She angled her face and closed her eyes as she rose onto her toes.

Before her lips could touch, he pulled away from her. She staggered forward a step without the support of his chest under her hand. He reached out to steady her and immediately released her.

"I dinna require anything of ye for my aid," Drake said vehemently.

She closed the distance between them again and slid her hand over his collarbone, up his strong neck and behind his head where his hair was surprisingly silky. "I know."

He stiffened. "I'm no' like those other men, Greer."

"I know." Her fingers toyed with his hair as she smoothed her other hand back over his chest, which rose and fell with his quickening breath. "Kiss me."

His heart raced with a frenzy under her touch. "Greer..."

But though he offered protest, he did not withdraw from her again. She tilted her chin, and their lips whispered against one another.

The yearning inside her caught her in a merciless grip then, demanding more. Her hand glided up from his chest to his jaw as her lips parted and fitted to his more firmly.

His mouth was soft, sensual, and intoxicating as his lips moved against hers. Desire thundered through her and echoed in her ears as the lust racing through her veins left her arching against him.

Aye, she wanted this kiss. More than that, she wanted this man, to slowly tear down his staunch rules and get him to lose control.

The same as he was doing now to her.

୧୬୬

THERE WERE MANY MISTAKES MADE THAT NIGHT.

Drake shouldn't have gone to Greer's room. He shouldn't have let her touch him. He should not have allowed her to kiss him. And for certes, he should not have kissed her back.

Lust roared through his body, his control barely tethered as his mouth claimed hers, again and again, their tongues brushing as he gave an audible groan. Greer clung to him, her hands clasped around the back of his neck as though she thought he might back away.

And truly, he should.

Though clearly, he wasn't doing anything logic screamed at him to do.

His hands glided over her slender waist, wrapping around her, fitting her more snugly against him. She leaned into him, her stomach nudging against his groin where his prick was swollen with a need he had too long denied himself.

His hand fisted in the rough homespun cloth of her kirtle in an effort to keep his wits about him. He wanted nothing more than to flex his hips against hers so their pelvises could meet in a grinding intensity that would further stoke the flames of their lust. Except he didn't. With every thread of willpower, he managed to maintain his control.

Greer arched against him, moaning softly into his mouth. Each whimpered sound crumbled his resolve a little more. If she continued thus, he might not be able to hold back any longer.

He caught her hips, intending to stop her, but instead, his hands followed the undulation of her hips, guiding her directly to the throbbing pulse of his arousal. She sucked in a breath at the contact and kissed him more deeply, her excitement evident in every lick, every little affectionate nip.

She grabbed his hand and put it over her breast before he realized what she was doing. "Touch me." Her breath was hot and sweet where she panted against his ear.

He should have withdrawn his touch, but the fullness of her breast filling his palm made doing the right thing impossible. She pushed herself against him, encouraging him with the way she ground their bodies together and with every breathless gasp of pleasure.

Her nipple pebbled beneath his touch, coaxing the teasing of his fingers. God, how he wanted it to be his tongue instead.

With a growl of resignation, he gently tugged at the neckline of her kirtle, freeing her breast for his hand to touch skin to skin and his mouth to close over. Her nipple was rose pink against her alabaster skin, its center drawn tight with anticipation.

He cupped the silken weight of her in his palm as he bent over and flicked his tongue over the nub.

Greer cried out, and her fingers raked up into his hair, keeping his head where he was at her bosom. As he loved her one breast with his mouth, he fondled the other before bestowing upon it the same attention.

His cock was hard as stone, shoving against his trews, desperate for the release he denied himself so often.

His was a life of control. Not of whims.

Her hand traveled down his abdomen and curled around the column of his arousal. The shock of it made his body lock up as his cock lurched in appreciation, straining toward the heat of her palm as she began to caress up and down over his hard length.

"Greer," he ground out. He meant to tell her to stop, but the words would not emerge.

"Touch me the way I'm touching ye," she whispered hoarsely.

He hesitated, aware that if he did as she asked, there might be no way to stop for either of them.

"Please," she whimpered.

His blood was too inflamed, his mind too far away from his grasp to deny her. He ran his hand up her leg, dragging her skirt with it until the whisper of petal-soft flesh teased at his fingertips. She trembled under his touch and mouthed the word "please" once more.

It was a request that was impossible to refuse. He continued up her leg to the sweet juncture between her thighs, where he gently swept a caress against her sex. She cried out in pleasure as his fingers came away damp with her arousal.

A low, rumbling groan rose in his chest, the sound desperate.

He was a man who prided himself on his control, of his body and his mind. Now both were being pushed to their limits, and he found his hold over them wavering.

Greer's hand on his arousal became more insistent as she rubbed the outline of his thick cock with her cupped palm, her breath coming in frantic gasps as his fingers glided over her ready sex. It was all Drake could do to keep himself from snatching her into his arms, tossing her on the bed and sinking into the tight, wet heat of her.

His heart thudded in wild beats that threatened to pound out of his chest. He pulled her more snugly against him, his fingers moving over her sex, finding her bud and caressing her with a quick, circular motion. Her knees buckled, but he held onto her firmly as he loved her with his hand. He reveled in every gasp, every moan as he watched the bliss play out over her face.

It didn't take long for her brows to flinch together and her cries to pitch with her climax as her sheath spasmed against him. He kissed her to quiet the sounds of her pleasure and did not remove his hand from her until her eyes opened.

She grasped the ties of his trews and tugged at them, but he stepped away with a shake of his head. "Drake," she gasped.

He clenched his teeth to regain his resolve. It would be so easy to allow her to free his arousal, to draw him into the tightness of her body, primed for coupling, to take her fully.

But no. He was not that man.

"Nay," he said, his determination firmly in place. "I'm no' like those other men, Greer."

"That's why I want ye. Because ye look at me with respect, because rather than hurt me, ye want to protect me." She reached for him, her slender, chapped hand palm up in an invitation that was more tempting than he cared to admit.

"I canna," he said gruffly and left her room. Before his will could splinter.

In the hall, light streamed up from the staircase leading to the tavern below. He remained outside her door for a moment, breathing in a deep, calming breath. Even then, his hands fisted on either side of him.

He took swift, quiet strides back to his own bedchamber, where he basked in the dark silence that greeted him. His emotions had controlled him once before in his life.

Anice.

Golden hair. Lovely blue eyes. A keen intelligence that people failed to notice when blinded by her beauty

His heart had beat its rhythm to the sound of her name for his time as Captain of the Guard at Werrick Castle on the English side of the border. Even after he had stood as the best swordsman for her marriage to another man. Even after he watched her slowly fall in love with her husband.

He had learned to wrest the power of his sentiments into submission then. If he had not, the ache of losing her might have been too great.

There had not been another woman who plucked at his resolve after Anice. At least, not until Greer.

Her feisty spirit, her sharp mind, the woman he knew her to be when her façade fell away, as exemplified by the way she gave to a child when she had nothing. It was in these ways that she chipped away at his fortitude.

And though he was tempted to embrace the whisper of those emotions, so too was he afraid.

He could not allow himself to suffer a broken heart again. Not when it could be so easily avoided.

❧ 10 ❧

All of Greer's plans slipped from her thoughts that night. She should leave, venture off on her own to steal enough to buy her brother's freedom. And yet, she could not bring herself to go.

Never had a man looked at her as if she were a person of value. Not like Drake, who had given her pleasure without seeking his own in return, putting her needs above his.

Mayhap she could trust him with her need to free Mac. The very thought set her heart slamming in her chest. It was such a great risk, and yet...and yet he might be able to help.

Wouldn't it be better to convince him to lend her the coin, or to find a way to earn it? Perhaps he could get her a job at the castle to pay off the borrowed amount?

Her heart lifted with more hope than she'd allowed herself in far too long.

After all, he continued to say that he meant to protect her. Wouldn't that include her brother as well?

It was with that thought in her mind that she slept soundly through the night, only waking when sunlight limned the slats of the shutters. She rose with exuberance, eager to face the light of a new day. To see Drake.

Her cheeks burned, recalling how he had touched her and brought her to climax with his large, capable hands. She wanted him to caress her thus again, to set her body on fire for him again.

Never had she allowed herself to even harbor any interest in a man before. Now, she was practically giddy at the prospect of seeing him downstairs while they all broke their fast. She washed her face and left her hair loose as she knew most men seemed to prefer.

She floated down the stairs and found Drake and Bean at the same table where they'd supped the night before. Joining them, she sat beside Bean and beamed at Drake. He gave her a half-smile that lifted the corner of his lips. It was boyish in a charming, endearing sort of way and set her heart knocking against her ribs.

"Are ye feeling better?" Bean asked.

She turned to the lad in surprise. "What do ye mean?"

Bean looked up at her with concern. "I heard ye moaning."

Greer pressed her lips together and intentionally kept her gaze from Drake lest she erupt into laughter. "The stew." She grimaced. "I think the bit I had might have turned. I'm much recovered now, but 'tis kind of ye to look after me."

The worry lifted from his expression, and she tousled his hair. "How did ye sleep?"

He shrugged and tore off a hunk of bread. "Well enough. My da always says no bed away from home is nearly as comfortable, and while I agree with him, mine was quite fine last night." He shifted his focus to his food, no longer broaching the topic of any sounds that might or might not have come from her room.

Finally, she locked eyes with Drake, but any mirth on her lips died at his fierce expression. She shook her head to indicate Bean didn't know anything, but he only frowned in return.

Damn.

They finished eating swiftly, as happened with three hungry souls prior to a long journey.

"Beathan, will ye see to the horses?" Drake asked.

The lad ran off with a grin. Drake waited until he was out of earshot before speaking to Greer. "I'd like to speak with ye privately."

Her pulse stumbled, then raced to catch up. Surely, he would relax once they were alone. Mayhap he'd draw her into his arms and kiss her senseless again. Possibly touch her, draw the pleasure from her body with teasing circles.

She led him into her room and turned to face him, determined to kiss the frown from his lips.

He stepped back. "I shouldna have stayed last night." He swallowed.

"I dinna mind." She stepped forward.

"I do," he said firmly. "What we did…" He shook his head, his jaw locked. "It shouldna have happened."

His words were like a slap, stopping her dead in her tracks. "Ye regret it?"

She held her breath as he studied her with those dark eyes that she'd spent all night dreaming of.

"I lost control," he replied after a long pause.

She reached for him. "I liked it."

"It canna happen again." His voice was resolute.

Rejection.

Her heart, which had only recently softened for the first time in her life, had been left vulnerable, fragile. His declaration put that hardened shell back up, protecting what should never have been laid raw.

"Dinna worry," she reassured him as she lowered her hand from his person. "It willna happen again."

He stared at her for a long moment before turning away. When he got to the door, she couldn't help the words building in the ache at her chest. "I thought ye said ye meant to protect me. Did ye mean for these three days of travel and nothing more?"

He hesitated where he stood under the assault of her questions. "I'm no' my own man, Greer." When he finally spoke again, his words were heavy with regret. "I have to remain at Lochmaben."

She'd known the truth of it from the first, that their time had to be fleeting. And for a little while, it had been enough.

Before she'd allowed herself to want more.

He might have been a reiver once, but now he was on his way to becoming a knight. And she was merely a peasant who had to steal to afford the bribe needed to free her brother from prison. A thief.

Now, she was glad she hadn't trusted him with Mac's secret.

"I know," she bitterly said when he didn't answer. "Ye're on yer way to become a knight."

"I would still protect ye," he said, so quietly she almost didn't hear him. He looked over his shoulder. "If ye were at Lochmaben as well..." He shook his head. "I still dinna even know where ye're going."

His unasked question hung in the air between them like a challenge.

"South," she answered.

He nodded, more to himself than to her, and quit the room, leaving her in resounding silence. It was too late to depart on her own now. Not when Bean would stop her and give her those sad eyes like a wee pup.

She should have known better than to have fallen for the likes of Drake, with his high morals. His casual manner in dismissing her left her bruised in a way no one had been able to inflict for some time.

An exaggerated sigh huffed from her lips as she hastily plaited her hair, then crammed her few remaining items within her bag.

There was nothing for it but to travel to Lochmaben with them and figure out what to do from there.

Bean and Drake were waiting for her when she arrived at the stables. Drake's deep red tunic made his black hair stand out against his tanned skin and dark eyes. He hadn't had time to shave, and a shadow hovered over his sharp jaw. It gave him a rugged quality, and she couldn't stop herself from wondering what it would feel like to kiss him thus. Would it rasp against her chin, a delicious contrast to the softness of his lips?

She steeled herself.

Damn him for looking so handsome.

"Drake says we'll arrive in Lochmaben by this afternoon," Bean excitedly said as he mounted his horse.

"This afternoon." Greer looked pointedly at Drake. "How wonderful."

His brows furrowed, but still, he reached a hand toward her to assist her onto the horse before swinging up behind her. If bearing witness to Drake's impossible attractiveness wasn't already enough to nudge her mind to what she ought not to be thinking, it was nothing compared to the familiar spiciness of his masculine scent.

He smelled like slipping control, like stolen pleasure and a quiet tryst. Her heart might be locked against him, but her body was melting at the recollection such scents evoked in her memory and made her ache to rediscover them once more. To go beyond their sensual petting and truly join together as one.

It was all she could do to keep her back stiff in front of him once more, especially when she wanted to arch her lower back, to push her bottom into his groin and tease them both for the duration of the journey.

They could not get to Lochmaben fast enough.

THE JOURNEY TO LOCHMABEN WAS INTERMINABLE. DRAKE'S arms were practically creaking with stiffness by the time the castle came into view, its boxy curtain wall visible from a distance. In front of him, Greer sat rigidly, her hair braided once more. Not loose as it had been that morning when she'd joined him and Bean to break their fast.

It was a small mercy that Drake was grateful for.

If her auburn tresses had been loose, the temptation would have been far too great to run his hands through them as he had the night before. To savor the sensation of the cool, silky strands slipping through his fingers. To breathe in her delicately floral scent.

Far too often, the passion they'd shared played out in his mind on that long journey. Not only the way she had softened in his arms and how she'd cried out with her exquisite release. It was also the way she had bared her soul to him and had listened and appreciated things he had never shared with anyone else. They understood one another in a way few did.

That realization made him want to curl her against him and hold her tight.

I thought ye said ye meant to protect me.

Something in his chest pinched. He did want to protect her. But how could he when she was to continue on, and he must remain at Lochmaben? Unless...she stayed with him.

He quashed the idea as soon as it entered his thoughts. Doing so would be far too dangerous. Her effect on him was not only physical but also emotional. The loch on the left reflected the open sky above, the choppy surface catching and sparkling with the sunlight like precious gems. He shifted his focus to the stretch of water, centering his mind on the gentle lapping of its waves against the narrow shoreline. At least until the long stretch of a wooden fence appeared on their right where the village beyond bustled with so much activity that any sounds of nature were completely drowned out.

Once they passed through the tall wooden gates, the castle was visible along the rear of the village. The portcullis was raised, and beyond it, the lowered drawbridge led the way into the fortified area for merchants and citizens alike. All along the battlements, red flags whipped in the breeze like dragon's tongues.

The structure was well prepared for an attack, as was evident by its unmarred appearance, especially when one considered the number of onslaughts they had endured in the previous years.

They were finally at Lochmaben. Greer would now be left to go off on her own.

Fear gripped Drake's heart. For what might happen to her without him there to protect her. For the times she would inevitably encounter a man who would seek to take advantage of her—for the one time she might not be able to defend herself.

He leapt down from the horse and held his hand up to her. She gazed down at him for a long moment before setting her fingertips to his palm and allowing him to assist her from the height of his destrier.

"Do ye think the guards will require our help immediately?" Bean asked from behind him. "There are many souls in this village. I'm pleased we're here to ensure their safety and survival. I think my da will be glad I've been sent on this mission."

Greer glanced to the lad and then shared a smile with Drake, as endearing parents might do with one of their children. But almost as soon as it touched her lips, she looked away, hiding her face. "I should be on my way," she said.

"Nay." The protest slipped from Drake's lips before he could stop it.

She returned her gaze to him, blinking in surprise. "Why?" she asked, wary. "Why should I stay?"

Because the thought of her leaving was unbearable. Because he longed to explore what they had begun the night before. Because as much as he was afraid of what she did to him, he still craved more.

"'Tis late," he said. "Ye would be traveling on open roads at night."

"And ye want to protect me?" she asked bitterly.

Aye, he did. For this night and all nights. But he didn't say that. He couldn't when it was nothing that he could promise.

"I'll pay for yer lodging and yer fare," he said. "For as long as ye remain at Lochmaben."

She scanned the village. "I'll stay only this one night. I dinna want ye to regret anything."

Her barb struck home.

He stepped toward her, their proximity intimate. "Greer..."

"Master Fletcher, we must go," Bean called. "Lord Calver will be awaiting our arrival. Greer, I'll ask if ye might dine with us at the castle tonight."

She gave the lad a tight smile.

"Ye'll stay tonight?" Drake asked for reassurance.

Greer nodded.

It was better than nothing, he knew, and one less night she would be at risk.

"Ye promise?" he asked.

"I promise no' to leave ye." With that, she waved him off and ventured out toward the village.

He hoped it wasn't her intent to steal. And if indeed it was, that she would not be caught. Bean took the reins of the destrier and Brevis, leading both horses toward the open castle gates and where they would meet with Lord Calver.

The guards on either side of the castle entrance stopped them. "What is it ye want within the castle?"

"This is Master Fletcher," Bean said in an authoritative tone as he displayed the king's missive with the royal seal. "He's been sent by King David to assist with the training of the new guards. It is imperative he speaks with Lord Calver at once."

The men's focus shifted from Bean to Drake, their gazes assessing. Drake bore their scrutiny with little concern, confident in his strength as a warrior. If they found him wanting in any way, they would alter their opinion upon seeing him fight.

Finally, they moved aside and granted Drake access to the bailey. Bean clicked his tongue for the horses to trot forward, and their footsteps thudded over the lowered drawbridge. Moments later, the sun was blotted out by the impossibly thick walls of the castle as they strode through the entryway, which spat them out into the open courtyard as Bean guided the steeds to the stable to be tended, and Drake waited for him near the entrance of the keep.

Drake's thoughts shifted to how he might best engage with Lord Calver and begin the subtle questioning about Lord Androll's daughter. Though Drake hadn't wanted Greer to be a distraction, he realized at that moment that this was the first time he truly had considered his role at Lochmaben Castle and how he might fulfill the king's request. It was a topic he ought to have been considering for the duration of his travel.

Now that they had arrived, he needed to devise a plan and quickly. After all, if he failed, he would lose this precious opportunity to become a knight.

And he knew without a shadow of doubt that he would not be given another chance.

11

Drake waited for Bean to join him. The lad scampered toward him—half attempted decorum, half unbridled energy—and led the way, his small chest lifted with pride for his role in the king's mission.

The Great Hall was longer than it was wide, the crossing beams overhead grand where they formed a pointed roof overhead. Voices echoed around them, softened mildly by the rushes spread underfoot. At the far end of the room was a raised dais where a man and woman sat in two regal chairs with ornate carving. Lord and Lady Calver.

A frisson of excitement flickered through Drake. This was truly the start of his mission. One in which he knew he would succeed. He had to, to finally be the kind of man his father would be proud of, to be victorious despite all the failures he had endured, to rise above the low acts he'd stooped to in order to survive.

Back straight and stiff, Bean approached the dais to deliver the king's missive to the earl and announce Drake. The earl looked at Drake with interest and waved him forward.

Drake obediently approached the stately figures, stopping just before the dais where he bowed.

"Master Fletcher," Lord Calver said in a clipped tone. "So, the king finally deemed it important enough to send a warrior to train all the new soldiers he's sent me. Most are so bloody green that they'd shite themselves before even thinking to pull their blades." He regarded Drake closely. "Let's look at ye then."

Drake lifted his head, forcing himself not to narrow his eyes at the soft-bellied noble who would so degrade the men who risked their lives to keep him safe. Lord Calver's appearance was well-matched with his whiny tone. His scalp was visible beneath his dark hair, and his face might be lined with a map of wrinkles, were it not so fleshy and his beard not so great.

The man's blue eyes bulged as if the fullness of his face were forcing them from their sockets. "Ye dinna seem verra large. I was expecting an exceptional warrior."

"He looks large enough to me." Lady Calver's voice was barely audible.

Drake flicked a glance at her in time to see the quirk of an appreciative brow in his direction as she reached for her goblet. She was younger than her husband, as was often the case with aging earls. Her golden braid was pinned around her head, and her deep brown eyes glided down his body as she lifted the chalice to her lips.

Lord Calver either did not notice his wife's comment or did not care. "Can ye fight?" he barked.

"Aye." Drake didn't bother to elaborate. His presence by order of the king was surely proof enough, even for a pompous noble. It wasn't Drake's job to recommend himself.

Though now he did understand why Lord Androll had his doubts on the story he'd been given regarding Lady Eileen. There was an oiliness about Lord Calver that put Drake's hackles up.

The earl scoffed. "We'll see how well ye can fight." He waved a servant closer. "Have their rooms prepared." His focus went to Drake once more. "Ye start tomorrow at noon."

Drake gave a single, firm nod.

Most nobles would have at least allowed him a day to refresh from the journey. But in truth, Drake didn't need the time to recover. He'd simply wanted the additional time with Greer.

His thoughts slipped back to her, to his fear that she would depart, and he would not have the chance to offer his farewells. Or mayhap give her whatever coin he could spare to keep her from having to steal to live.

Or possibly kiss her one last time. To taste the sweetness of her lips. Something to hold tight to for the rest of his life, for he knew after tonight, he would never see her again.

"Ye may go." Lord Calver made a shooing motion with his hand.

Drake bowed and took his leave.

"He dinna seem verra grateful," Bean muttered under his breath. Fortunately, the lad had waited until they were at least out of the Great Hall before sharing his opinion.

Drake discreetly shook his head to silence the lad from saying anything further. "Walls have ears in such places as these," he said quietly.

Bean's eyes went wide with understanding, and he pressed his lips together.

A woman strode in front of them, and Drake put his attention immediately to her, first to assess her distance to gauge if she might have heard Bean's comment. But then, recognition took hold.

A petite woman with an impossibly slender waist and her pale blonde hair pulled back in a series of braids that fell into gentle curls at the ends.

No sooner had he realized who she was than the woman turned back to him, her blue eyes lighting with her own recognition, and a brilliant smile blossomed on her lips.

"Drake?" she asked in a breathy voice.

"Lady Anice," he said in return. "Lady Graham," he corrected, using her married name.

She cried out in delight and rushed toward him with the grace that most noblewomen could only dream of possessing. She threw her arms around him and squeezed, then stepped back with a laugh. "Forgive me, I know you don't enjoy such affection, but it's been an age since I've seen you. And I certainly didn't expect to see anything to remind me of home here." She cast a disgusted look over his shoulder, her dislike for the earl and countess apparent in her expression.

"'Tis good to see ye," Drake said earnestly. And indeed, it was.

He had imagined this moment countless times, a chance meeting with her where her husband was not around. An opportunity to be alone with her. Or at least as alone as one could be with Bean standing nearby, his watchful stare taking everything in to likely comment upon later.

Yet in the times Drake had fantasized about meeting her, his heart had thudded like a blacksmith's hammer against his ribs, his blood going hot as sin in his veins as he imagined confessing to her everything he had never dared say. His undying affection for her, the way he had loved her with every part of his being.

But now his pulse remained even, his blood temperate and his tongue held not with restraint, but truth. It struck him like warm sun on an icy day.

He didn't harbor romantic affections for Anice anymore.

"What are ye doing at Lochmaben?" Drake asked.

"James has to meet with each of the March Wardens from time to time to reassure them he hasn't lost his Scottish loyalty despite our living on English land." She waved it off as though meeting with the earls who controlled the Scottish border was something of little concern, though she knew the matter to be of great import for certes. "We don't mind the other two, but Lord

Calver is always rather unpleasant. I didn't dream of seeing you here. What brings you to Lochmaben?"

"I've been asked to help train the new guards," he replied easily.

She threaded her hand into his arm. "Do tell me how you've been all this time. Have you found yourself a woman?"

A grin spread over his face, one he couldn't stop even if he wanted to.

She gave an excited gasp as they continued to walk onward. "You must tell me all about her. Is she here? I would so love to meet her."

He shook his head, a feeling of shyness suddenly washing over him. Not only with Bean giving him an odd expression that promised a stream of questions to answer to later, but also for fear of scaring off Greer.

For that was truly all he could think of in the time since he encountered Anice so unexpectedly—Greer. Her smile, the way her green eyes held his, how she smelled so wonderfully of flowers, the way she kissed and tasted and loved.

At that moment, he realized that no matter how much he had tried to erect walls around his heart to keep himself from caring for her, he had failed terribly. He wanted Greer in the way he had once wanted Anice.

Nay, not in the same way.

More.

And while such a revelation ought to have frightened him, the idea of accepting that he loved her suddenly felt like home.

THE CASTLE ROSE BEFORE GREER, OMINOUS WITH WHAT IT represented. Her brother lay within the bowels of the dungeon there. No doubt, a few minutes' walk would bring her right in front of him if she were granted entry.

But she wouldn't be. Mac was in there, and she was outside, standing in the sunshine with a full belly and clean clothes.

She chastised herself where she remained, loitering near the castle gate like a lost pup, waiting for Drake and Bean to emerge. She originally had planned to pick a few pockets while they were detained inside the castle. But as she reached for the first one, her usual calm was offset with a tremor of fear.

Usually, she did not worry about being caught, not when she could typically talk her way out of it. Except now, instead of only fearing what might happen to Mac if she were taken prisoner, she worried also about Drake. And how his association with her might cost him his dream to become a knight.

She was becoming too damn soft.

Now she hovered by the entrance in anticipation of spending an evening with him before departing to figure out a way to free Mac. All too soon, she would be swept into her former life again, where her meals weren't guaranteed, where protection was at her hand and where she was never afforded a modicum of respect.

Footsteps thudded over the drawbridge. Greer glanced in the direction, eager to see Drake. A woman's delicate laugh tinkled through the air as he came into view with a lovely woman on his arm.

Nay, not a lovely woman—an exquisite woman. Jesu, how was it possible for a lass to be so bonny? It was hardly fair to the rest of the women in Scotland to compete against one so stunning.

Something ugly and painful tightened in Greer's gut as she took in the extent of the woman's beauty. Pale blonde hair, blue eyes, full lips, and white, straight teeth. She moved with such grace that it appeared as if she floated over the drawbridge rather than walked as mere mortals must do. Men's gazes followed her, mouths opening in gaping awe, and she paid not a mind to one of them.

Nay, her entire focus was on Drake, her hand curled daintily against his strong forearm.

Whatever had gone soft within Greer now set hard as stone. She remained where she stood in the shadows, scowling as they basked in the golden light of late afternoon together.

The woman laughed again and said something to Drake as she pulled her arm away. He glanced about, his gaze finding Greer as he waved her over. She clenched her hand into a fist at her side and slowly approached, confirming what she had already suspected—the woman was even prettier up close than she was from a distance.

So bloody unfair.

No sooner had Greer stepped out into the light than a shadow blotted out the late sun beside her. She glanced up and found a beast of a man striding past. He might be the tallest man she'd ever seen. Certainly, he was the strongest, with bulging forearms and powerful shoulders. His copper-colored hair was pulled back in a leather thong, and his nose was slightly crooked on his face, as though it'd been broken a time or two.

"James." The woman reached for the man as he approached her and Drake, then stretched on her toes and gazed lovingly up at him before kissing him.

The man had a besotted look on his face that reverted to sternness once more as he turned from her and reached an arm toward Drake. "'Tis good to see ye again, my old friend."

"How is the bairn?" Drake asked.

"Ach, the lad is four summers now." The massive man beamed, clearly a proud father. "Thanks be to God his looks come from his mum."

"Oh, do stop." The woman pulled her husband to her before catching sight of Greer. "And who is this?"

Greer wanted to melt into the ground. She was no one in the face of this beautiful noblewoman with her fine attire and finer appearance. By comparison, Greer was a pauper in rags, not to be spared a second glance.

"This is Greer," Drake offered. "Greer, this is Laird and Lady Graham."

"Oh, but do call me Anice, please." Lady Graham smiled openly at Greer, without malice or condescension.

Who was this incredible woman?

Laird Graham inclined his head respectfully to Greer as well.

It was all too much. These respectable people treated her as if she were worth more than the homespun cloth on her back.

"And I'm Beathan." Bean stepped forward and gave a broad smile that revealed his large front teeth. "Master Fletcher's squire."

"Well met, Beathan," Lady Graham said sweetly in such a manner that it left the lad blushing furiously.

A servant emerged from the castle, leading two saddled horses toward them. "Alas, we must be off," Lady Graham said regretfully.

"We canna leave fast enough," Laird Graham said in a low voice, meant only for their party. "Lord Calver is a shite excuse for an earl."

Bean grinned up at the laird. "I told ye," he said triumphantly to Drake.

There was a round of farewells after that as the couple mounted their horses and were on their way. Greer did not miss the final wave Lady Graham tossed over her shoulder to Drake, nor how he watched the woman as she rode off.

Hot pain twisted in Greer's chest, a discomfort she could scarcely stand. Whatever the terrible sensation was, she knew it to be put there by her affinity for Drake and for the woman he still cared for. A woman the likes of which Greer could never compete against.

"I canna stay," Greer said abruptly. "'Tis why I met ye here. To tell ye I'm leaving."

Drake and Bean both spun back to her.

"'Tis almost dark," Drake said as Bean whined, "But ye said ye'd sup with us in the castle."

"Beathan, have them secure three places for us," Drake instructed.

The lad hesitated, looking between the two of them before slowly slinking off in compliance, his slower than normal pace indicative of how he felt about being sent away from the conversation.

Drake moved closer to her. "Greer, stay."

He was so near that the subtle scent of him teased at her with reminders of the intimate moments they had shared. Her head spun with a heady, airy sensation that made the pain in her chest burn with greater intensity.

She had allowed him to elevate her to a station she had never belonged. One of respect.

Now she was right back down where she always had been. Except she had never realized how truly low that had been. Nor how much she had craved being better.

She glared up at him. "I'm no' a dog."

He shook his head. "I dinna mean it like that. I meant..." His words tapered off.

"Ye meant what?"

Those deep brown eyes met hers, the affection there evident. And it sliced at her insides like a sharpened dagger.

"I mean, I dinna want ye to leave." He reached for her hand. "No' tonight. Nor any other night."

Her gaze went from where his hand held hers to back up to his face to gauge the earnestness of his statement. "Ye're asking a lot," she said slowly.

He smiled, his expression so charming, it tugged at her heart. Drake was not the sort of man to try to win a woman over with a smile. In fact, he was not the type of man to attempt to win a woman over at all. "Supper, at least. Though I canna say that I want ye alone out in the dark..."

Greer didn't want to be out there in the darkness either, but nor did she want to stay and continue to have her heart battered by a man who could not uphold promises to protect her, promises that weren't his to keep. Especially not when she had to unearth a way to gather the considerable amount of coin she needed for Mac's freedom.

"Aye," she finally answered. "But only for supper."

Mayhap getting into the castle would present an opportunity to get to Mac on her own. There had to be something she could plan with being so close.

❧ 12 ❧

Excitement fluttered through Greer's stomach as she strode into the entryway of the thick, fortified stone keep. It was a prospect she did not intend to squander.

Now that she was inside, she could assess the layout herself. Surely, no one would fault her for getting lost in such a large place. A need for the garderobe at some point would allow the perfect occasion.

Mayhap she could even locate the dungeon on her own and actually see Mac. Her pulse kicked up with anticipation, the rush of it so intense that it made breathing difficult. A month and a half had passed since she had last seen her brother. The possibility of being able to do so soon released the rush of emotions she had pushed down for so long, allowing them to rise forefront and making her eyes prickle with hot tears.

"Are ye well?" Drake asked as he led her toward the open doorway of the keep.

Greer wiped at her eyes, feeling suddenly foolish. "Aye, of course. 'Tis only a bit of dust."

He did not appear reassured but did not press her further as they entered the Great Hall.

Greer swallowed her surprise at the magnitude of the massive room. In all the years she had lived on the outskirts of the village, she had never been inside the castle. Her steps slowed as she took it all in, awed by such splendor. The tapestries appeared glossy with their carefully stitched silk threads, the colors vibrant from dyes available only from distant lands and winking with precious bits of gold and silver thread. Flagons of ale were set upon each table with matching salt cellars and various bowls and platters. Even the trestle tables were lined with linen.

How was it even possible for a man who wasn't a king to have such wealth? To display such opulence while so many went without?

Bean rushed over to them. "I was told we were having boar tonight. Come, yer seats are this way."

"Our seats?" Greer asked. "What of yers?"

"I'm sitting with the other squires." His grin indicated he was not at all put out by the prospect of him spending time with lads his own age. "But ye're a guest of import." He lifted his brows at Drake.

As they walked farther up the lines of trestle tables, near the front where several knights sat, unease twisted in Greer's stomach. She didn't belong here, at the front of the room, garnering attention.

If she'd realized she would be in such a place of observation, she might have tried to find a fresh kirtle or mayhap have done something more with her hair. Her cheeks burned as people turned to watch them pass until they were finally at their seats. Not at the front, but near enough to leave her nerves ragged.

Drake did not appear upset by how very much she did not belong among such fine people. Once they were seated, those who had watched them appeared to lose interest and turned their attention to their meals and conversations.

"I've no' ever had boar," Greer admitted sheepishly as a servant brought over a platter and lay it before them. Steam rose from the pile of roasted meat. The skin was cooked to a lovely, crisp gold.

"'Tis quite good." Drake sliced off a hunk and slid it on her plate. "I would like ye at the table with me every night if ye did decide to stay."

"I..." Greer bit her lip.

Drake frowned and regarded her. "What is it? Are ye expected somewhere?"

"I..." She folded her hands in her lap, hating this newfound uncertainty. "'Tis complicated."

A servant came by with a flagon of wine. The liquid that splashed into their cups was a deep crimson, the aroma rich. Greer took a sip, expecting the sharp vinegar taste she'd experienced before. The decadent spice of this wine rolled over her tongue like velvet and left a pleasant warmth as she swallowed it down.

"Fifty marks?" Drake asked.

Greer nearly upset her wine in her surprise. Though she managed to catch it in time, a bit of wine sloshed over the rim and dotted the white tablecloth. She guiltily edged the bottom of her chalice over the stain to hide its existence. "What did ye say?"

"Ye asked me once for fifty marks," he said. "While it might no' have significance, I think it does."

Her heart hammered in her ears. Years of learning to maintain a calm façade, even as panic threatened to unravel her, her hand remained steady as she cut into the piece of roasted boar on her plate. "Why do ye say that?"

The meat was juicy, briny with seasoning that seemed to intensify every time she chewed. There weren't any bits of gristle or bone or even fat. Just lean, delicious meat.

Drake glanced about as though ensuring no one appeared to be listening in on what he said. "I dinna think ye steal without purpose."

Greer lifted a brow in silent indication for him to go on.

"Someone who can easily talk a merchant out of no' one, but two pastries need no' steal for her food." Drake held his goblet but didn't drink from the vessel. "When ye received coin for returning the gold belt, ye pocketed it. Except when ye saw the wee beggar, ye gave it up to the bairn without a second thought, which means some things matter more to ye than wealth. And then, there are yer hands."

Greer curled her hands in her lap. Drake lightly ran his touch over her clenched fingers with one hand and sipped his wine before returning the chalice to the table.

"Ye're no opposed to working hard for yer keep." Drake's brow furrowed. "Until now. Something happened to make ye need more than laundering could provide."

Greer's heart banged about in her chest with an agitation that made it too hard to breathe. Too hard to think.

How could he know her so well after only a few short days? How could he so easily read every aspect of her life when she had worked so hard to keep those parts of herself carefully hidden?

"Am I wrong?" he asked.

Greer didn't answer. How could she when he was so unerringly correct?

He moved her wine to place it in front of her, revealing the red stain on the white linen. "I want to help ye, Greer. I wish ye would tell me why ye need it, but I dinna want to force ye."

She drank from the wine, scarcely tasting it this time, merely wanting the numbing effect of the alcohol to calm her frantic pulse.

"If I gave ye fifty marks, will that help ye?" he asked when she set her goblet aside. "So ye dinna have to steal again."

She pulled in a deep breath.

Fifty marks.

Without having to lift it from people's pockets or worrying about what being caught would mean. She and Mac could return to their quiet life in the hut by the loch, where she took in laundry from their neighbors, and he played innocently in the sunshine.

Tears pricked her eyes.

She nodded tightly, unable to speak past the knot in her throat.

"I'll get it for ye after the meal ends," Drake said.

She was quiet for a long moment, in awe not only of his assessment but the way he had ascertained the extent of her need. He not only respected her, but he also saw her as she truly was—beyond the façade that she put up. Whatever mask she wore for others, he saw through it. He knew who she was and understood why she did what she did.

And he still wished to help. To protect.

She glanced up at him, this handsome man whose heart was entirely pure and perfect—someone who had rescued her when no one else would have ever cared—and something inside her chest broke open.

༺✿༻

THE AMOUNT OF COIN THE KING HAD GIVEN DRAKE FOR TRAVEL had been generous. With the expenses of travel, there were about fifty-five marks remaining. Giving Greer the fifty marks would not leave him much. However, Lord Werrick, whom Drake had spent years working for as Captain of the Guard, was not so far off over the border. Mayhap, if need be, Drake might get a loan to compensate for the funds he was offering to Greer.

It made Drake's gut knot even to consider having to ask to borrow coin, but the look of wondrous relief on Greer's face lessened the stress of such a possibility.

"Thank ye." Her whispered gratitude was almost inaudible against the backdrop of noise around them, the various conversations and laughter, the scrape of eating daggers over the pewter plates and bowls.

He wanted to ask then if she would stay in Lochmaben for good, but it was not his place. Not after he had offered her so much coin. If she stayed, it should be of her own volition and not because he had paid her to do so. He would not save her in one moment to make her feel as though he had purchased her in the next.

"I'm glad I could help," he said with genuine feeling. "I truly meant it when I told ye I want to protect ye."

She nodded and turned her attention to her plate once more, carefully eating, though he could tell from her distant gaze that her thoughts were far removed from where they sat in the Great Hall at Lochmaben Castle.

Her reaction only further proved his suspicions about her need for that exact amount, and he was grateful he was able to give it to her.

When they had finished eating, and the servants were collecting the last of the platters, Drake knew the night had drawn to an end.

"If ye'll wait here, I'll go gather my purse," he said.

Greer shook her head. "I'd rather go with ye." She glanced about, her cheeks reddening. "I dinna want them to think I'm a pauper who snuck into the castle and try sending me on my way."

There it was again, the evident discomfort she'd exhibited when they first entered the Great Hall. It made him ache to see how her confidence chipped away when faced with those of greater means than herself. As if she thought them better people simply because their purses were heavier.

Drake hesitated. "If ye're seen coming to my room—"

"I dinna mind." Her gaze flicked about them, and she gave a wry smile. "I'm sure most here would expect it."

That made him even more inclined to deny her request—at least until she put her hand to his forearm and said in a quiet voice, "I'd like to speak with ye alone as well."

"Aye," he agreed reluctantly. "But follow several paces behind me."

She nodded in agreement, allowing him to rise from the trestle table and leave the room first. The corridor beyond the massive wooden doors was dark by comparison, only lit by several flickering sconces rather than the numerous candles that illuminated the large area within the Great Hall. He walked slowly to ensure she shadowed his path, not turning any corners or going up any flights of stairs until he knew for certain she was behind him. At last, he came to a stop before his bedchamber. His pause was intentionally long to indicate which door she was to enter. To be certain, he left it slightly ajar upon going inside.

She entered behind him a moment later. Her cheeks were still flushed from the glass of wine she'd had, and her auburn hair curled elegantly alongside her face. She gave him a shy smile as she entered his room. Her apparent reticence stirred something within his chest.

He closed the door behind her and lowered the bar to ensure they wouldn't be interrupted. She might not have a care for her reputation, but he did.

The longer she remained in his bedchamber, the more at risk they were of having someone try the door. Especially when Drake hadn't asked Bean where he was sleeping. Not wanting to waste time, Drake went to a drawer and withdrew his leather purse. He plucked a few coins from the top, knowing exactly how many overall were within, and offered the purse of the remaining coins to Greer.

She stared at it for a long moment. Her eyes welled with tears, and her chest rose and fell with her frantic breath. "Are ye certain? 'Tis truly a great fortune."

It was a fortune. Even to him, who had acquired much wealth in the last few years. That she didn't take for granted the impact of such coin, even for him, was appreciated.

Rather than tell her yes, he took her warm hand in his and gently placed the purse in it.

"I hope ye're no' in any trouble," he said. "But if ye are, ye can come to me." When she didn't answer, he tried again. "Mayhap, that's what ye wanted to speak with me about..."

She bit her lip and shook her head. "I know ye regret last night. I know I'm no' a lady like yer friend Lady Graham, nor anywhere as—"

"I regretted it because I dinna want to besmirch yer honor," Drake said. "No' because of who ye are. I like who ye are."

Greer sucked in a quiet breath. "Ye do?"

"Verra much," he admitted. "I canna stop thinking about ye."

"I'm just a peasant." She looked down at her feet. "A thief."

He caught her hands where they cradled the purse in his own. "No' anymore. Ye dinna need to steal. Ye can have an honest life."

"Do ye love Lady Graham?" she asked abruptly.

Her question took Drake aback, and he found himself scrambling for what to say. He didn't love Anice. He knew that now. But for several years, he'd thought himself very much in love with her.

"Nay," he answered with certainty.

"Ye hesitated in replying." Greer folded her arms over her chest, appearing suddenly uncomfortable. "She's verra beautiful. I dinna know a woman could look like her."

As transparent as Greer was to him, so too was he to her, apparently.

"She is lovely," he confessed. "I used to think she was the bonniest lass I'd ever seen."

"Used to?" Greer's brows lifted. "Ye're telling me there is a woman even more stunning than her?"

"Aye." Drake grinned. "Ye are."

Color bled into Greer's cheeks, and her fingers went to her braid, nervously twisting it. "I'm nothing compared to Lady Graham."

"Anice is her own person." He gently pulled Greer toward him, gazing down at her.

She came to him easily, her eyes locked on his.

"And ye are yer own person," Drake said. "Ye could no' ever be 'nothing.' Especially no' to me." He caressed her soft cheek, and she turned into his touch. She needed the truth, no matter how foolish he felt saying it aloud. "I regretted what happened last night because I care about ye too much—because I'm afraid I'll somehow lose ye."

"Drake." She reached for him. He did not draw away. At least not until her eyes closed as her mouth lifted to his.

He backed away then, fearful that if he kissed her, he might not be able to stop. Not when his body still roared with desire for her after the night before. He'd seen to his lust, his body so primed, it had taken only several hard, fast pumps of his fist before his release overtook him. Now though, he was as randy as an adolescent, his cock already swelling at the prospect of kissing her.

She looked questioningly up at him.

"I should go secure a room for ye in the village." He moved toward the door.

"Or ye could stay here." She followed him to the door. "And I could stay here as well."

13

Greer realized she had been wrong about so many things. Drake had regretted the previous night out of respect for her, out of fear he'd lose her. Then there was Lady Graham and her impossible beauty—yet he thought Greer was lovelier. Such a thing did not even seem possible, but he'd said it with such sincerity and affection in his dark eyes that she couldn't not believe it.

Certainly, she could not allow herself to long for him as she did if his heart belonged to another.

But it did not.

Quite the opposite, it seemed.

The prospect of such a thing left her feeling heady.

But not so much that she forgot her original purpose for requesting to come to Drake's room. Being in the castle was an opportunity she could ill afford to squander, especially with the fifty marks resting in her purse. It would be far easier to approach the guard while she was within the thick stone walls. The last time she'd entered the castle, she had to use deceit to gain her admittance—a story about looking for a fictional husband who had gone to see the earl and had not returned.

This time she wouldn't have to try to convince someone to let her in.

Her location inside the castle was half the battle already won. Having the coin was the other. Such weight for such a slight bag!

But then, she imagined it was fitting for a purse of such heft to be worthy of a lad's life, of his freedom.

If she could somehow find the soldier tonight, the dark-haired man named Tavish, she and Mac might wake up the next morning in their own beds, in the small hut beside the loch. They could have their life back, pretend as though none of this had ever happened.

Except that she would never forget Drake. Her heart tugged at the thought of leaving him. Of never seeing him again.

It was on the tip of her tongue to tell him about her brother. Except Drake was there to train soldiers and surely that did not include instruction on accepting bribes. She couldn't do anything to jeopardize the one guard who could guarantee Mac's liberation.

A knot of tension squeezed at the back of her throat, but she forced it down. Now was not for crying. Now was for celebrating this incredible man, for cherishing the incredible gift he had given her. It was a night for him.

For them both, together.

"Drake." She went to him, blocking the door this time. "Let me stay with ye tonight." Her hand went to his chest, stopping him even as she reveled in the strong warmth of his body under her palm.

He didn't move from her touch, and she remained where she stood, savoring the feel of him. A true warrior. One who looked at her now with the soft gaze of a lover.

"I've never been in so fine a room," she said shyly.

It was true. The chamber within was far more luxurious than any room she had ever seen outside of the Great Hall of Lochmaben Castle. Not only was the room itself large, but so were the furnishings, with two carved chairs set before a fire, and a bed whose posts stretched up to the ceiling where a canopy draped over the structure. Those heavy, crimson curtains that hung on all four sides would cradle them in obscurity, so their entire world would be only one another.

"I'll sleep in the village," Drake replied, as obdurate as ever.

"Nay, I want ye to sleep here. With me." She ran her tongue over her bottom lip, recalling the sensation of his mouth on hers. "I havena been able to stop thinking of ye."

His gaze flicked to her mouth, and his nostrils flared slightly. He knew exactly what she referred to.

"I want ye to kiss me again," she whispered. "Touch me again, make me come undone again—as ye did before."

He shook his head, tensing. "I dinna give ye the money for this—"

"I know." And she did. However, that he gifted her the money was part of the reason she was doing it. Not out of obligation, but out of appreciation for the man he was, out of gratitude that he saw beneath her façade. And she did it out of affection, for the way she couldn't stop recalling his touch, his kiss. The way he had ignited her blood.

The coin was a considerable sum, especially to someone who had nothing. And regardless of what his social standing might be now, for most of his life, he'd had nothing. He knew what he gave her and asked for nothing in return.

Her chest warmed at such generosity—that someone would do something like that for her. Her heart, which had opened to no one but Mac, parted now for Drake.

It was dangerous and thrilling and exciting. She wanted to fall headlong into this feeling and embrace it completely. With him.

He shook his head again. "Ye dinna owe me—"

"I know." Then, she pushed up on her toes and kissed him, capturing his mouth with her own, teasing her tongue between his lips to allay any protest.

She didn't know what would happen to them after Mac was

free. If anything *could* happen between them, or if their worlds were too far apart, too complicated to join together.

What she did know was that she could have this night with him, which was more than she'd ever dreamed she'd want. She would not squander such a gift.

The instant he succumbed to his longing for her was evident in how his muscles relaxed beneath her hands and his fingers threaded up into her hair, loosening her braid.

"Greer." He groaned her name and paused kissing her to study her face. "Ye're so verra beautiful."

She gazed up into his eyes, lost in their dark depths. "Love me, Drake."

He kissed her again, this time taking possession of her as she had with him, branding her with the force of his desire. Greer's blood ran hot in her veins and thundered with longing between her thighs, the memory of last night's pleasure fresh in her mind.

And she wanted more.

Where Drake had been reserved previously, his actions now were sure. He cupped her bottom with a firm grip, fitting her pelvis against his with their layers of clothing between. Still, it was not enough to mask his hard prick. Never had she thought such a thing would ever be welcome.

Now she knew exactly how welcome it could be, how it made her knees go weak, and her sex twitch in anticipation.

His leg nudged between hers as he offered his strong thigh for her to stroke her body against. The sensation was exquisite and led to a breathy gasp from her lips, which he caught with eager, delicious kisses.

Her hands roamed over his warrior's body in an exploration of the carved ridges of his physique. She lifted the hem of his tunic, desperate for the heat of his skin beneath her palms. Distractedly, he yanked it over his head and tossed it to the floor, so only the thin leine he wore beneath separated his nakedness from her greedy touch.

It was not enough.

With a hungry whimper, she dragged the hem of the leine higher. At last, she jerked it from his torso, this time unveiling his glorious strength as she did so. The firelight played over his powerful frame, not hiding anything, each well-honed muscle flexing and shifting with the slightest movement. Truly, the man was a sight to behold.

And it was only fair to return the favor. She set her fingers to the rough leather laces that bound her kirtle in place over her breasts and, as she watched him, slipped it free.

⚜

DRAKE COULDN'T TAKE HIS EYES OFF GREER AS SHE TUGGED THE ties of her kirtle, her bright green eyes fixed on him. The leather gave a little pop as it came undone, followed by the drag of the coarse ties through the homespun cloth. Her fingers were graceful as they moved over the lacing, unraveling it until the bodice began to gape open to reveal her white chemise beneath.

The breath caught in his lungs as the garment loosened enough to expose her smooth shoulders, almost concealed beneath a curtain of her silky red hair. He should stop her, put an end to this before it could begin. But his blood was on fire, his cock solid as stone, his mind too hazy with lust.

She swept both chemise and kirtle down her arms, baring her firm breasts and pink-tipped nipples. An ache clenched through him to drag his tongue over the taut buds once more, to make her cry out.

Lower the garment went, revealing her narrow waist and the divot of her small navel, then down even farther over the swell of her hips to reveal a triangle of red hair above slender, perfect thighs. The kirtle fell away, and she straightened, naked and indescribably beautiful with her skin gleaming like a pearl in the candlelight.

Drake let a rare curse slip from under his breath.

Warm color spread over Greer's cheeks as she stepped over her discarded clothes and reached for him. "I've no' ever heard ye say that word before."

His gaze skimmed over her once more as she gracefully stepped closer, her body lithe and sensual. "I've no' ever seen a goddess undress before."

"No one has called me a goddess before." Her arms slid over his shoulders and curled around the back of his neck, so her breasts stretched higher on her chest. Chills skittered over his skin, so delightful he nearly groaned.

"The world is full of fools." He enfolded his arms around her, caressing her silky, cool skin and drew her against him. Her breasts pressed to his chest, and her willowy form arched into him, to where his cock raged against his trews.

A low growl escaped him, and he lowered his face to hers to claim her lips. All the pent-up longing broke free at that moment, with their naked skin gliding against one another as their kisses became deeper, more frantic. Their hands roamed over one another's bodies as they learned each other's exquisite shapes.

Her fingernails skimmed over his skin in her exploration, sending fresh waves of goosebumps while her mouth eased down his throat to his earlobe that she caught gently in her teeth, sending a huff of her warm breath against his ear. His hands smoothed down her waist to the flare of her hips, which he fit against his pelvis, so the friction of their grinding bodies teased them both with every undulation.

Drake kissed down the column of her throat, trailing lower to her breasts. Greer tossed her head back with a gasp and arched her torso toward him, her nipples already rosy and tight with desire. He caught one bud in his mouth and flicked his tongue against it in a way that made her writhe in his arms.

His fingers descended beyond her delicate navel to the thatch of hair. Her breath came faster as she read his intent. He glided a fingertip along the seam of her sex, and her knees buckled, causing her nearly to collapse.

In a single motion, he swept her into his arms, carried her to the bed and nudged aside the heavy curtain with his elbow. He lowered her gently to the bed and crawled over her. Her chest rose and fell with her lusty pants as she watched him, her eyes bright with anticipation and lust.

He kissed her mouth first, enjoying her with his lips and tongue—as he intended to do with the whole of her body. She tried to rise onto her elbows to deepen their kiss, but he shifted downward, pressing his lips to the column of her graceful throat, and tracing the line of her collarbone with the tip of his tongue.

She sucked in a breath and began to lie back as his mouth descended to her breasts once more, and his hand glided over her sex. Her legs parting to give him better access as he probed her lightly with his finger while his tongue teased over her nipple. She whimpered with little cries of pleasure, each one encouraging his hard cock that now strained with such force against his trews, he thought he might go mad with wanting.

"Please, Drake," she gasped. "I want ye."

I want ye.

The words were an invitation to heaven. One he ought to decline. If he were as good and honorable as he tried to be, he would satisfy her with his hands, then cradle her in his arms as they slept.

But hadn't he been good and honorable long enough?

Could he not take this one thing he wanted, this woman who did something to his heart as much as she did something to his body?

Before he could find the words to protest, he shifted off the mattress and tugged at the ties of his trews. His cock burst free, jutting out with a readiness he could not hide.

Greer squirmed on the bed, rubbing her thighs against one

another in anticipation. Drake shoved his trews down his legs and approached the bed.

She lay there on the mattress with her auburn hair shimmering against the deep crimson coverlet, her eyes bright with longing, her cheeks flushed. God, she was beautiful.

His.

Aye, he wanted to make her his.

He moved over the top of her, and she spread her legs, shifting beneath him so his erection clumsily bumped against her sex. Bracing himself on one arm, he took his cock in hand, angling it toward her center.

And hesitated.

This was the one moment where he could stop. Where he could do the right thing.

But he did not.

He plunged into her in a single thrust, burying the pulsing force of his prick into her tight, wet sheath. Her grip on his phallus was far too intense, and her body went rigid, her eyes wide with surprise.

God, he'd hurt her. But he didn't understand...

She blinked up at him, tears in her eyes. "Forgive me."

Understanding dawned and in that instant, he realized the depth of what he had done. What his lust had cost her.

"Greer," he said raggedly. "Ye're a..."

A tear ran from her eye. "Was. A maiden, aye."

❧ 14 ❧

There were many reasons Greer had not wanted to tell Drake she was a maiden prior to their joining. Even still, in this moment when he remained frozen over her —his body locked and rigid, his gaze wounded—she regretted her omission.

He tried to pull away, but she held onto him regardless of the way the small movement stung at her center. "Dinna go," she begged.

He shook his head, his eyes haunted. "I shouldna have..."

"Ye dinna know." She curled her legs around his waist to secure their bodies together more firmly. "And 'tis already done."

"I hurt ye." He caressed her face. "If I'd have known..."

"If ye'd have known, ye'd no' have had me at all." It was one of the reasons she hadn't told him.

He didn't reply, which she took as confirmation that she was correct.

"'Tis already done," she said again.

His brow furrowed, his expression anguished.

She shifted her hips upward, nudging their joined bodies together. There was some discomfort in doing so, but she knew it would pass. Peasants didn't soften stark truths by bandying about niceties the way nobles did. Greer knew well what to expect when she lost her maidenhead. And Drake was the man she wanted to give it to.

He was the only man she would ever deem worthy, the only one who would likely be kind about the process.

"I wanted it to be ye." She searched his gaze. "Ye're the only man who has ever looked at me with respect, the only man I—" She was saying too much. Instead, she shifted against him despite the additional pinch around the foreign feel of him inside her. "Touch me, please."

A muscle worked in his jaw, but he ran his hand lightly down her body, leaving a wake of pleasant chills in his path as he found the little bud nestled in her sex where their bodies joined. The contact was as a flash of lightning to her system, instantaneous and thrilling.

"Aye," she whispered. "Like that."

She moved under him as he brought fire back into her blood with his ministrations, and as the seconds passed, the soreness gave way to the first tingles of pleasure. A gasp passed through her lips with surprise and delight.

Drake's fierce expression relaxed somewhat, and he carefully drew his hips back as his finger circled over the highly sensitive nub. A tease of friction rippled wonderfully through her. She leaned her head back with a moan.

It was then he truly began to love her, first with careful flexes of his pelvis until they were both groaning with restraint and then with hard, aggressive thrusts. Greer held onto him while the maddening flickering touch of his finger worked over her as he pushed within her.

Suddenly, it was more than she could take. The tightening in her body snapped, and she cried out at the exquisite waves that swept over her. Her release was magnified from what it had been before, her pleasure continuing to climb as Drake's pumping increased in speed until, at last, he jerked against her. He ground out a roar, and every muscle flexed in an appealing show of strength and lost control as his release overtook him.

His cock spasmed inside her as he spilled his seed and clung to her, his heart thundering against her own. The pleasure of his climax within her left Greer gasping with the enormity of her fulfillment.

They remained clasped in one another's arms, staring into each other's eyes in wonder as their breath calmed and their erratic pulses slowed to a steady rhythm.

Drake's dark eyes were fathomless, something Greer felt herself tipping into, eager to lose herself in it forever. Her body was languid from the force of their loving, and her mind was more at peace than she could ever recall it having been before. She wanted to stay in this moment for the rest of her life, where she was loved, where she was happy, where she was safe.

But she couldn't. Not when Mac was still in the bowels of the castle.

The realization was like a splash of cold water.

Drake pressed a kiss to her lips. "Marry me, Greer."

She stared up at him incredulously. "Do ye jest?"

He withdrew from her and lay at her side. "Nay. I want ye to be my wife."

Her confusion at the sudden question was short-lived when she remembered who this man was at his core—one of chivalry and honor. And she was the maiden he had deflowered.

"Ye dinna have to do that." Heat scorched her cheeks.

"I want to." He didn't say it with vehemence, as if a man agreeing to a mission. He said it tenderly, like a lover. Like a man who meant every word.

Her heart crumpled in on itself.

It was so tempting at that moment to agree to his request, to imagine herself on his arm, dressed in a fine gown, visiting the nursery in their manor filled with bairns. All their bellies full, and their hearts light—together.

"My da is dead," she said. "Ye've no angry father to come after ye." She meant it as a joke, but it fell flat in the quiet room.

Because she wanted to agree, to live the life she envisioned in her mind. Free from hunger and fear and loneliness. But she couldn't. At least not yet. Not until she had rescued Mac.

Unease knotted in her stomach and warned her it might not be as easy as she anticipated. She hoped it was just fear affecting her thus. And how could she not be afraid with so much at stake?

"Ye dinna need to tell me yer answer now," Drake said quickly. "Think about it and give me yer answer, aye?"

Greer nodded. Hopefully, by the time he asked again, Mac would be home, and she could explain everything without fear of losing her opportunity to save her brother.

Drake drew her into his arms and held her against him, embracing her in warmth and strength. She savored the safety there in his embrace, with the leather and spice of him mingling with the sensual aroma of their loving. Exhaustion pulled at her, promising a sweet and blissful sleep.

But she had to slip out tonight to find the guard.

She remained where she lay long after Drake's even breathing told her he was asleep. Staying awake had been torture when she wanted nothing more than to melt against him but holding sleep at bay was necessary. If she gave way to slumber, she wouldn't wake until daylight touched the room.

Nay, Mac would not spend another night in the dungeon.

She regrettably withdrew herself from Drake's arms and silently pulled her clothes on, her gaze fixed on him to ensure he did not rouse. He looked young with his face so tranquil in slumber, the hard lines of the life he'd endured softened by sleep. It made her ache to climb across the mattress and kiss his sleep-warmed lips.

Heart heavy, she quietly took up the purse he'd given her with the fifty marks and slipped out the door.

❦

A WHISTLED TUNE BROKE THROUGH DRAKE'S SLEEP. HE'D SLEPT deep enough that he wished to linger a little longer. The bed was soft and comfortable, and he was not due to watch the castle's guards train until noon that day.

He rolled to his side, his hands reaching before his mind even recalled why.

Greer.

He peeked an eye open but didn't see her lying at his side. The night before played back vividly in his mind. Every detail, sensual and tender alike.

He had asked her to marry him. Contentment warmed his chest.

He had asked her to marry him.

Granted, she hadn't agreed to wed him, but he'd allowed her time to think about it, lest he frighten her off like a skittish deer. The whistling in the room continued.

"I dinna think ye'd be up so verra early." He finally opened his eyes and grinned as he pushed himself onto his forearms.

Bean grinned at him and gave him a cheerful wave. "Good morrow, Master Fletcher. I actually slept a mite later than usual. The door appeared locked last night." He turned to the heavy wooden door of the bedchamber with a slight frown. "But then when I checked back later, it wasn't. Mayhap it was stuck." He shrugged without concern. "I dinna get to bed until late as a result."

Drake looked discreetly around the room for Greer. Bean would have said something if he'd seen her, for certes. Even as Drake glanced frantically about, he couldn't help the flicker of guilt at having locked poor Bean out of their room.

But where had Greer gone?

"I thought ye'd go to the village with the other squires," Drake said cautiously.

Bean froze. "How did ye know they went to the village?"

"I'm no' so old that I dinna remember such things." Drake sat up in bed, recalling his youth when he'd wanted to be a squire, back when his da had been alive, and the possibility of being a knight was not some far-off dream.

Drake and the lads had been thick as thieves as they scoured the village for whatever trouble could be found. He'd been only an observer himself but knew how it went about regardless. And what it was like to be the moral outlier.

"Have ye seen Greer?" he ventured cautiously.

"Nay." Bean turned his attention to Drake's chainmail in his lap, his hand hovering over the linked metal where he held the oiled polishing cloth. "I dinna stay out with the other lads. They dinna like me."

"They dinna know ye," Drake protested.

"Even the ones that have tried to get to know me." Bean sighed and rubbed at a spot on the chainmail. "'Tis why I was sent with ye. To get me away from the other squires. And the knights. They dinna like me either."

Drake regarded the lad for a moment, his chest tightening for him. Even now, Drake still struggled with people who did not care much for his virtues. It was the kind of thing Drake would ordinarily approach Bean about and put a reassuring hand on the lad's shoulder...except that beneath the sheets, Drake was entirely naked.

"'Tis hard to walk the line of justice when so few see its purpose," Drake said from where he lay beneath the safety of the sheet. "Especially among those who should hold honor above most."

"Ye too?" Bean looked up, his eyes wide. "People dinna like ye either?"

Drake scoffed and shook his head. "I dinna much care for them, myself."

Bean grinned. "Me neither."

It was Drake's turn to offer a casual shrug. "Then why fret about what they think?"

Bean nodded to himself. "My da has said the same to me before as well."

"The chainmail is already well-oiled from when ye did it last time, lad." Drake indicated the caul in Bean's hands. "Will ye see to bringing up some ale and pottage? Today will be busy, and we will need sustenance."

"Aye, of course." Bean hopped off the stool and practically ran from the room, leaving Drake blessedly alone to wash and dress with haste. The last thing he needed was Bean questioning why he'd slept naked.

Greer's disappearance, however, consumed Drake's thoughts.

Where had she gone?

Now that he was alone to think it over, unease curled around his gut. Had she decided to leave the village after all? Had she traveled all night?

His pulse quickened. What if she had been attacked? What if she was injured?

He tugged on his chainmail in preparation for meeting the guards on the battlement for practice when his door swung open and clicked closed. "I hope ye were able to find a bit of bread as well. I'm hungry as a beast—" He turned around to greet Bean and fell silent.

It was not Bean standing beside the closed door. Lady Calver tilted her head with interest at what he was saying, her expression bemused. She wore an elegant gown the color of blood with flecks of gilt thread that dotted the silk in a pattern like stars.

"Braw men always do have insatiable appetites." She arched a brow.

"I thought ye were someone else." He stiffened into a soldier's stance. "Forgive me, my lady."

"There's no' anything to forgive." She smiled coyly. "Relax."

But he did not relax. Having the lady of the castle in his bedchamber could implicate him in a way that would compromise his entire mission. Destroy all his dreams.

"Is there something I can assist ye with, my lady?" he asked.

Her lips curled up in a smile. "There is." She walked around him, inspecting him the way one might a horse at market. "Ye appear hale and hearty. A fine representation of a man."

He said nothing, not liking where this was going.

"My husband has many mistresses." She let the statement hang in the air like a suggestion.

A sudden thought jarred through Drake. "Including yer ladies-in-waiting?"

The coquettish expression on her pretty face remained, but her eyes went hard. "Why would ye ask that?"

"They seemed the likely source," he answered smoothly. "Are we no' having a discussion that invites the opportunity for questions?"

The muscles of her slender neck flinched. "We are. But it isna my husband I'd like to discuss. 'Tis ye." She stepped closer. "I can satisfy ye better than the peasant woman ye came upstairs with last night." Her gaze slid toward the bed where the sheets were still tossed about as if she could read what had happened there.

Drake took a step back. "Forgive me, but she is all I need." He kept his gaze distant, past the noblewoman lest she take his direct eye contact as interest. "I intend to marry her."

"Do ye fancy yerself in love?" She gave a hard, bitter laugh. "Ye'll find such things foolish and a waste of energy. When yer heart is broken, and yer cock is hard, come find me." With that, she spun away from him and swept from the room.

Bean entered a few minutes later with a tray of bowls of

pottage, a few eggs and two mugs of ale clutched in his hands. He sniffed the air. "It smells like perfume in here."

The lad missed nothing.

Drake didn't bother trying to explain. Not when the lad would only ask more questions. Instead, he sat at the chair by the fire and indicated the seat opposite him. "Let us make haste with breaking our fast. I want to arrive in time to see the guards train." So he would know what he had to work with. At least for the mission that Lord Calver assumed him to be there for.

What Lady Calver said about her husband's mistresses dug at Drake's thoughts. It was obvious from her reaction that Drake had been correct about Lord Calver's affairs with her ladies-in-waiting. Lord Androll's daughter had been one of those ladies-in-waiting.

The idea of Lord Calver with a young woman brought on a shudder of disgust.

But some women were drawn to power. Even still, all options would have to be exhausted before Drake rested his assumptions on the Earl of Calver. Not when the man was of such incredible wealth and his support to the crown so important.

Such accusations would not be taken lightly. And if incorrect, there was no recovering from such a fault.

For now, Drake needed to set his sights on appearing to train the guards while subtly finding any additional information he could on Lady Eileen's death.

And, of course, figuring out exactly what had become of Greer.

🦋 15 🦋

Greer huddled deeper among the piles of soiled linens as the shadows of passing footsteps flickered along the light at the bottom crack of the door. The small room had been a poor place to sleep, especially in comparison to where she could have been in Drake's arms.

Her heart wrenched.

He'd been in her thoughts all night, not only because of the way he had made her body feel, but also because of his offer. Marriage. It rolled around in her head until it was smooth as a loch stone. And never did it lose its appeal.

Her sacrifice of a precious night at his side had been in vain. Tavish had not been on duty, at least not based on the men she had passed. She'd slipped through the castle, unseen in her futile efforts. It was good that Drake and Bean were there to encourage their training as the men truly were in sore need.

Which might well work in her favor, for she would not leave until Mac was with her.

Footsteps stopped in front of the door, and her pulse froze.

She had meant to wake before dawn, to slip out and find

somewhere else she might hide or to try to blend in with the staff as they moved about the castle. Surely with so many servants, she could easily disappear among them.

But exhaustion had held her cradled among the pile of dirty sheets until far too late. By the time she'd roused, it was to the clatter of large buckets slamming to the hard, stone floor outside.

All at once, the doors swung open and light flooded in, momentarily blinding her.

"Ye lazy slut," a woman hissed. She grabbed Greer's arm in a painful grip and hauled her upright.

Greer's knees were stiff from inactivity, and she stumbled a step before catching her balance.

"Ye knew we were understaffed this morning, and here ye are sleeping." The woman's reddened face announced her annoyance before the great huff she issued forth. "Nothing to say for yerself?" She put her hands on her hips. "Go on, then. Get the pile ye were sleeping on and start with washing them."

The woman jerked her head in the direction of the open room.

All around them were large barrels filled with sheets that billowed wetly over the milky gray water. Lye. Of course.

Well, better a task she knew than something she didn't, like cooking fine food.

Before she set to work, she took a strip of linen from a shelf and bound her auburn hair beneath it in the same fashion as the other women who rushed by. It wouldn't do to have one's hair dipping in the cloudy water or tangling in clean sheets.

And it certainly wouldn't do to get caught.

No doubt the new warrior in charge of training the guards would be on the lookout for a woman with long auburn hair. And she couldn't go to Drake until she had Mac.

The day passed in the humid air as she scrubbed and scoured at sheets with practiced expertise. With each move of her body, the weight of Drake's purse bumped within her pocket against her thigh, providing reassurance of its existence.

If nothing else, working in the laundry occupied her mind and hands rather than leaving her to fret over the possibility of not being able to find Tavish again that night. Without his aid, she didn't know how she would get Mac back. And if the Earl of Calver painted Mac as a thief—or worse—Drake would never support freeing him.

Nay, she wouldn't think about what would happen if she failed.

"Have ye seen the new warrior that arrived on the king's order to train the guards?" The woman to Greer's left said as she plunged her hand into a barrel of water and withdrew a linen chemise.

Thus far, their chatter had not drawn Greer's notice. At least, not until the mention of Drake.

"Ach, the dark-haired one?" another woman asked and grinned in obvious appreciation. Several others around them laughed.

"Those are some sheets I wouldna mind making dirty." An older woman gave a lascivious wink. "'Twould be worth the extra scrubbing."

Again, the ladies all laughed.

Greer kept her head down, focusing on her task as she had through the day. But she couldn't deter her thoughts from envisioning those tangled sheets she'd slipped from as she had left Drake's side.

He was a rare man. Not just for his fine appearance—and he was indeed remarkably fine—but for how good a person he was. Before having met him, she never would have assumed that someone such as him could exist.

She only hoped his goodwill would forgive her for having left him as she did. And for doing what she could to free Mac.

THE SOLDIERS' SKILLS WERE MORE LACKING THAN DRAKE HAD anticipated. Most scarcely appeared old enough to grow a beard, and more than a few were so old, they wobbled where they stood. The border had been hit hard by the war with England, bearing the brunt of the onslaught for years.

It was not the fault of these men that they were not proper warriors.

After holding them at practice longer than was necessary and showing them correct ways to attack and defend, he finally allowed the men to return to their posts.

"They'll need a lot of work," Bean said, his expression serious with evident concern.

Drake appreciated the obligation in the lad's tone. "I'm sure we'll be able to help them."

Bean nodded determinedly.

Drake's gaze skimmed the courtyard once more. Not that he expected Greer to materialize suddenly. That ache threaded its way back into his chest. "Have ye seen Greer?"

Bean's attention snapped to Drake. "Is she gone? Ye asked about her this morn."

Rather than deny it, Drake ran a hand through his hair. "I'm no' sure where she went. I saw her last night," he caught himself, "at supper. I've no' seen her since."

"I'll check the village. Which inn did ye pay for her room?"

Drake inwardly grimaced, hating to lie to the boy but refusing to admit the truth of what had happened. How they had shared an incredible night where they showed one another with their bodies what they were too afraid to say with words. How after proposing marriage, Greer had run in the middle of the night.

A simple nay would have sufficed.

His gut clenched. "I dinna know which one she's at. I simply gave her coin to go to one of her choosing."

Bean did not appear to realize Drake was not being truthful and instead looked out over the battlements to where the village sprawled below them. "She could be anywhere down there." His small mouth screwed up in thought. "Ye stay here and search," he announced with the decisive nature of a commander. "I'll search the village."

"'Tis a good way to go about it." Drake squeezed the lad's shoulder. "Ye'll be a fine leader someday."

Bean grinned with pride. "I'll no' let ye down. If she's there, I'll find her."

Drake didn't doubt Bean's ability to locate her, but he did question her even being within Lochmaben at all. Hopefully, a few questions might aid him in discovering what happened.

He approached the guardhouse first.

The two men within, both lads barely older than Bean, leapt to attention, their eyes darting about the room as if in a final inspection to determine what failures they might be reprimanded for. The open shutters behind them showed a direct view to the drawbridge, the castle's only exit, as well as the wall beyond where one would enter—or exit—beneath the raised portcullis.

"Have ye seen a suspicious woman leave the castle?" Drake asked.

The two slid a glance at each other; both had light bruising under their eyes from exhaustion, having clearly been on watch all night.

"What is it?" Drake asked, his heart kicking up with anticipation that they might have seen Greer.

"D...do ye mean the lady?" the taller guard asked. "The one that died."

Drake kept his reaction steady despite hearing the reference of the woman whose death he must solve. "I might. Tell me what ye know."

The shorter of the two nodded to the other. "'Twas him who saw her."

The lanky guard nodded. "She rode out that day alone. Without even a guard. It seemed odd."

"Did ye mention it to anyone?" Drake asked. "About it seeming odd."

The lanky man immediately appeared chagrined, and the other one nudged him with his elbow. Finally, he sighed and continued, "I tried to bring it to Lord Calver's attention, but he wouldna hear anything of it. He said she broke her neck riding her horse, and that was the end of it. I thought ye might come to ask, being as ye're new to the castle."

"We'd hoped ye would," the other piped up.

It was on the tip of Drake's tongue to ask what the lanky man felt about being told Lady Eileen's death was a simple, immediate end but decided not to press too hard lest they grow suspicious. Instead, he nodded with a very Bean-like authority.

"Have there been any other lone women departing the castle, specifically at a late hour?" Drake asked.

The men glanced at each other and shook their heads. "We've been here since the middle of the night."

Once Drake had left the guardhouse, however, he pointedly left his questions with the other guards vague in an attempt to lure as much information on Lady Eileen as possible. But while many guards said they saw Lady Eileen leave alone on the day her neck was found broken in the field—and several seemed suspicious of the circumstances of her demise but did not elaborate—not a one had seen a woman depart in the middle of the night.

Which meant Greer was still inside.

But why? Why would she stay in the castle? Especially when she had the coin that she'd asked for.

It was a question he couldn't answer, but one he had a sinking feeling he needed to resolve.

However, after subtle questioning through the day, he was not any closer to locating her. Bean returned from the village, down-trodden with disappointment.

"I dinna find her," he said. "I tried so verra hard."

"I know ye did, lad." Drake put a hand to the lad's thin shoulder. "Go get some food, aye? I'll stay on with the guards tonight. Mayhap she'll turn up."

Bean nodded solemnly and trudged toward the Great Hall while Drake considered the enormous size of the keep. She was in there somewhere.

And he would figure out where she had gone.

❧ 16 ❧

As the day passed into night, Greer's limbs were heavy with exhaustion from a hard day's work. In truth, it felt good to work with her hands again, to not have to rely on theft.

The women she had toiled beside left for their homes in the village while she managed to slip away and hide in the shadows until everyone was gone. Between the efforts of her labor, a fresh meal still sitting in her belly she'd eaten with the other ladies and the residual heat in the workroom, the temptation of sleep tugged at her anew. She resisted the urge to close her eyes and forced herself to wait a good amount of time before emerging from the small room into the larger, open laundry area.

Only a shuttered window appeared visible in the rear of the room, allowing a seam of moonlight. She bumped her way around and quietly slipping out into the hall, where the wall sconces mercifully lit her way. But while she could see better, she knew that meant she could also be seen better and tried her best to remain in the shadows.

Tavish often patrolled the main floor of the castle, which was how she found him when she arrived at Lochmaben previously. He was working during the day then but indicated he was generally there at night, which played well to her advantage now.

Footsteps approached, and she blended into the shadows of a deep-set doorway, hoping it would be sufficient to keep her hidden. Men's voices filled the corridor, quietly conversing and chuckling as two soldiers appeared in front of her. They were engaged in their chatter as they passed, the one nearest to her close enough that she could have touched him.

And they did not notice her.

She exhaled a whoosh of air and slipped into the hallway once more. Her hand went to her heavy pocket to ensure the coins did not clink as she moved, her footsteps thankfully muted by the leather soles of her shoes. Moonlight streamed in from the open shutters and cast a silver pallor about the wide hallway. She darted from column to column, her gaze scouring the area for guards, both the ones she wanted to avoid and the one that she sought.

Finally, she caught sight of two men standing together, their voices a baritone murmur that drifted toward her. One possessed a similar posture to Tavish, who tended to slouch about the shoulders.

She cursed her luck that he would be with another person. But how to draw him away?

Fortunately, she didn't have to come up with a solution, for as she was mulling over her predicament, the other man gave a loud scoff and strode down the hall. The tightness in Greer's chest abated somewhat. Everything was working in her favor.

She quickly crossed over to where Tavish was turning to face the wall and arrived as a steady stream of urine splashed into the rushes.

"I dinna know if Lord Calver would approve," she whispered.

Tavish didn't startle. He glanced at her over his shoulder and grinned, revealing his broken front tooth. "I wager he's done it a time or two himself when a garderobe wasn't a stone's throw away."

Greer kept her distance and stared up at the high ceiling above them. Even in the dark, the crossing wood beams stood out against the whitewashed walls, making them look like the sticks game Mac used to play when he'd been little.

"I have what ye asked me to get." Her heart slammed in her chest as she said the words.

There was a jingle of his chainmail links rattling against one another as he tucked himself back into his trews and faced her. "It doesna matter. The lad is heavily guarded."

"He was heavily guarded before." Greer withdrew the sack of coins from her pocket and waved it in the air like a prize. "Surely for fifty marks, there is some way he might be released."

Tavish's eyes glittered with avarice as he watched the sway of the small purse.

"Ye can do it, can't ye?" Greer asked in a playful tone. "For me?" She hefted the purse. "For this?"

Tavish growled and shifted his weight with apparent aggravation. "It doesna matter how much I wish to. I'm no' daft enough to try it. Something changed today. Lord Calver put more men on the lad."

Something cold slithered down Greer's spine. "Why would he do that? What changed?"

Tavish's gaze slid away, and he shrugged.

"What changed?" She repeated.

"I dinna know."

"Ye do. And ye're no' telling me." It was an effort to keep her voice quiet, especially as a knot of dread tightened in her gut. She pulled a mark from the purse and tossed it to him. "Tell me."

Tavish snatched the coin from the air and quickly pocketed it. "After all this time, Lord Calver has made a decision on what to do with the lad this afternoon."

Greer pulled in air but still found it difficult to breathe. "What's to be done with him?"

"They're going to put the lad to death in the morn." He looked at her with a grimace, as if he were afraid of her and rubbed at the back of his neck. "Hanging."

The world seemed to fall out from beneath her feet. She staggered back, unable to find purchase.

"Tavish," someone shouted.

The guard hesitated, casting a regretful look at her.

She jerked her head to indicate he should go. They needn't arouse suspicion. Not now.

Mac was to be hanged. Tomorrow.

Unless, of course, she could do something to stop it.

An idea blossomed in her mind, wild and reckless and rife with determination. She would save him herself.

❦

DRAKE STRODE THROUGH THE DIMLY LIT HALLS OF THE CASTLE. The soldiers were even more relaxed in their duties at night than he'd seen during the day. Their conversations floated up from various corridors and around corners. Outside on the parapets, he'd even found two men asleep, their backs pressed against one another for the support.

Lord Calver might be a cruel and selfish earl, but he was correct in citing his need for someone to better train his men. Drake would ensure he reported that to the king upon the completion of his mission.

However, there was one benefit to their lack of discipline— they were not quiet about the goings-on of the castle. From what Drake understood, Lady Eileen had indeed been engaged in an affair with Lord Calver. Additionally, several people had seen her depart alone that afternoon on horseback. A strange thing for a lady. And clearly, a dangerous one.

By the afternoon, the guards appeared to be on edge about something. He approached two men walking side by side and snagged the last bits of one's statement. "I guess he finally decided what to do with him."

"With whom?" Drake asked in an innocent tone.

The man spun around, his eyes widening. "Eh?"

"Ye said, 'he finally decided what to do with him,'" Drake replied nonchalantly. "I'm asking who ye meant."

"Eh...my brother..." the guard stammered. "With eh...his son..."

A lie.

The same as all other inquiries Drake had made. Aye, something was amiss for certes. And he would get to the bottom of it. That, and deducing where Greer had gone. He was still convinced she hadn't left the premises.

A shadow shifted behind the men, immediately catching Drake's attention. "What was that?"

The men looked at each other, then followed Drake's gaze to the empty, shadowy corner. The guard who had lied about his brother shrugged. "I dinna see anything."

Drake narrowed his eyes. "Something moved."

"I dinna see anything," the other guard said, echoing the other man's useless sentiment.

Drake walked between them and went to the corner. The skin at the back of his neck prickled. There was something there. He'd seen it.

"I really dinna think anything is there," the first guard said.

Drake ignored him and strode down the hall. Moonlight teased over the rafters and across the walls, bandied about by the passing clouds. Nothing appeared out of the ordinary. But it hadn't been the night playing tricks on him.

He knew what he'd seen—someone was sneaking about the castle.

The guards didn't follow him as he went to survey the area. In truth, he preferred they stay put and leave him to it. There was no need for them to join. Their steps were too loud, and the volume of their conversation was as much an announcement of their presence as a drumbeat.

A slight sound came from the end of the hall, almost imperceptible as if the swish of cloth over stone. At the same time, the edge of a shadow slipped around the corner at the end of the corridor.

There *was* someone there.

Greer, mayhap?

He hastened after the shadow, his steps quiet from years of practice. But when he reached the stone stairs descending into the dungeon, he paused. If it were Greer, she would have no reason to go to the dungeon.

The ridiculousness of the situation was not lost on him. Greer most likely slipped from the castle without any of the foolish guards seeing her. Mayhap she was long gone now, and Drake was chasing shadows, imagining them to be her.

Although there *was* someone lurking about—of that he was certain—it was very unlikely that they had a good reason for breaking in to descend to the bowels of the dungeon. Drake had not been shown its location upon his introduction to the castle. And now, as the icy fingers of the underground area wrapped around him, a chill shivered down his spine.

If nothing else, he could discover more about the prisoner everyone had been going on about. The one no one would give him an answer on. Drake stepped off the final stair into a large room with not even a sconce to diminish the blackness. In a place that was all shadows and no light, it would be easy for the person to hide.

His eyes adjusted swiftly to the darkness, enough that he noticed a flash of movement. Without thought, he ran in the direction, giving chase.

Whoever it was, he *would* catch them and learn why they'd snuck down into the dungeon.

THE GUARD WHO HAD BEEN FOLLOWING GREER WAS QUICK, HIS movements so silent, she almost thought she had lost him until he began to run after her. Even then, his steps were quiet, his breathing even. He disappeared into the dark area as she did. Were it not for the clink of some bit of metal on his person, she might not even know he was there.

But he was there.

And he was getting too bloody close.

She raced across the open room, mindful of muting the sounds of her frantic fleeing to avoid alerting any other guards. Except the entire location was too unfamiliar to her. The room narrowed down to a locked iron door with bars set compactly together, nothing she could hope to squeeze through.

She darted to the left and met a damp stone wall, its surface slick with the mold of constant moisture. Her breath came so fast that surely her panting would lead the guard right to where she stood frozen in the grip of panic.

There was nowhere to go. No way to get to Mac.

Tears clogged her throat as she realized her defeat. There was nothing she could do for her brother tonight. Instead, she turned on her heel and raced back to the stone steps. Better to leave and find a way to save him in the morning rather than remain and be captured.

Hanged.

The word rumbled in her mind like thunder directly overhead, ominous and frightening.

Mayhap that was what had preoccupied her until it was too late—when she heard that last footfall of the other person, landing nearly next to her. Suddenly, the weight of a body slammed into her. The force of it was so strong, it knocked the air from her lungs and left her gasping for breath.

But she would not go down without a fight, not when her arrest would mean Mac's certain death.

Nay, she would fight with every last bit she had in her.

The body under Drake squirmed, a slender bit of nothing he might easily crush. Drake had knocked into them with enough force to send them both sliding over the damp, earthen floor of the dungeon.

His opponent managed to free an arm and slammed a fist into his jaw. The hit was one of desperation but not nearly strong enough to do much damage. Even still, the person fought with determination, their body wriggling with such vigor, it was nearly impossible for Drake to hold them in place.

It took considerable effort to get his body locked over the person and to grasp their skinny wrists in his hands. A knee came up at that point, jerking into Drake's crotch. He ground out a low groan and released his hold for a brief moment.

That was all the other person needed. They twisted away from Drake and attempted to dart away once more. Except Drake was too fast. He reached out in a final effort to capture the fleeing person, catching their ankle, and yanking it.

His opponent crashed to the floor and kicked at him, preventing him from holding their foot. Drake threw the full force of his body atop them to keep the person from running away once more.

The "oof" that emerged from the figure beneath him was decidedly feminine.

He froze.

The woman writhed beneath him, trying to free herself. All at once, he knew exactly who this woman was, whose deft skills would allow her to drift unnoticed through the castle for over a day, who would fight back with such tenacity, who would not reveal her gender upfront in a bid to allow herself to be treated softer for it. What he didn't know, though, was why.

He folded his hands around hers, recalling how only hours ago, they had learned the shape of the body he now had pinned under him. "Greer."

The woman stopped moving, and her breath caught with surprise. "Drake?"

His name was a whisper in the darkness, filled with shock and horror. He eased off her and made his way toward the wall where the outline of a sconce showed against the stonework. Using a flint from the pouch at his belt, he lit the rush nip, setting a golden light flickering through the cavernous space.

It was as he imagined the dark space in his mind—an open room with a barred door on one end that led down a corridor of cells.

"What are ye doing here?" he demanded.

Greer looked through the barred door to the row of cells. "Please let me go. I'm the only person who can save him."

Him.

Something dug into Drake's chest. Was there another man Greer cared for?

Only then did it occur to Drake that he had never asked her if there was anyone else.

This could be like Anice and James all over again, leaving his heart to crumple under the burden of unrequited love. Except this time would be far, far worse, as the extent of his emotions for Greer ran much deeper than those that he'd had for Anice.

Shouting was discernible from beyond the other side of the bars.

Greer grabbed Drake's arm, her grip like a vice. "We canna be here."

"Of course, we can," he protested. "I'm with the guards."

"No' with this prisoner. He's different."

"The light is coming from beyond the gate," someone shouted amid the thunder of footsteps.

In a huff, Greer blew out the light and tugged Drake toward the stairs.

"Ye always wanted my trust," she hissed. "I'm prepared to give it to ye fully, but I am asking for ye to do the same in return. We have to leave now."

Keys rattled in the barred door. The guards were coming.

Logic told Drake he ought to stay where he was, but something else entirely pulled at his heart and dragged his feet up the stairs. Greer continued to pull at him, not only up the stairs but into the dimly lit hall that she navigated with surprising ease as if she'd done it before.

At last, they stopped before a set of doors she pushed through. The harsh scent of lye soap clung in the air, and large, empty barrels filled the open space, highlighted by a sliver of moonlight. The laundry.

Before he could ask any questions, she hauled him to the back of the room and ducked behind a barrel blanketed by shadows, indicating he should do likewise. The slam of heavy feet sounded just outside the door. Drake ducked low, and the door flew open, bathing the room in light.

"No' in here," a gruff voice called out.

The door slammed closed, and darkness fell over everything once more. Ire rose in Drake, not only for the guards' ineffective search—for he and Greer should have been caught—but also the risk he had put himself in for her.

In that one moment, he might have sacrificed everything to help her. To help her lover if that was who this "him" was.

The thought made his insides clench.

He ought to have known better than to trust her, than to want this, than to have opened his heart again to the possibility of love, a future.

He frowned at her. "What is the meaning of all this?"

She looked over the barrel once more, confirming no one was in the room with them before putting her back to the curved wooden slats.

Moonlight trickled in around the outline of shutters against the far wall and filtered into the room. It was in that bit of silver-white light that her expression took on a look of chagrin. "I havena been entirely honest with ye."

Drake's stomach churned with dread, and his heart beat so loud, even the lackluster guards would surely hear it thrumming from behind the door. "What havena ye been honest about?" he asked through numb lips.

"What I needed the coin for," she said. "Why I left ye the other night, why I couldna reply to yer marriage propos-al." The last part was delivered so softly, it was nearly inaudible.

"Ye love him." Drake left it as a statement, not wanting her to answer for fear that it might forever wound his heart in a way that it would never recover.

Regardless of wishing she wouldn't answer, she did. "Aye, of course I do."

GREER'S MIND WORKED SO FAST THAT SHE COULD SCARCELY KEEP up. Part of it was due to how very nearly they'd been caught. Another part was the crippling fear of what would happen to Mac if she couldn't get to him. And then there was the fierce expression on Drake's face...

"I need yer help," she said gently. "My brother has seen two summers less than Bean. If I dinna get him out of the dungeon tonight, tomorrow, he..." Her words trailed off, unable to finish the grim reality little Mac would soon face.

A confused crinkle across Drake's brow smoothed. "Yer brother?"

"Aye, 'tis why I needed the fifty marks." She pulled the purse from her pocket and handed it back to him. "Less one for a bribe that dinna do anything more than give me dire news."

Drake slowly accepted the purse. The coins clinked against one another inside and echoed off the stone walls around them. "I need to know everything."

Everything...did they even have that kind of time?

With her gaze constantly flicking toward the closed doors, she explained as quickly as she could how she'd found the dead noblewoman and Mac missing, as well as how the guard had offered to help get him free for fifty marks and how she'd gone first to the king for help, but how she'd been refused an audience. She even admitted to her plan to steal on the journey back to pay off the guard.

"I found the guard again," Greer said. "But he told me there were too many others around Mac, and it would be impossible to free him before morning when...when they..." Her throat closed around what she meant to say.

"When they?" Drake lifted his brows.

Greer dragged in a shuddering breath. "They're going to hang him, Drake." All at once, the terror at what her younger brother faced swept over her, as well as how overwhelmingly helpless she was to save him. Hot tears streamed down her face.

In an instant, Drake was there, drawing her into the comfort of his strong, warm arms. She sagged against him, and the tears flowed before she could stop them.

It was an indulgence she couldn't spare time for, and within several seconds, she pushed away and wiped at her eyes.

"Why dinna ye tell me any of this before?" Drake asked.

She shook her head. "I was worried ye'd get me to confess who was accepting the bribe, and I would lose the opportunity to rescue Mac. That man was my only hope."

Drake ran his hand down her cheek, his gaze so tender it made fresh tears well in her eyes. "I'm going to help ye. Put yer hope in me, aye?"

Her heart skipped a beat. "Ye are?"

"I am." Drake hesitated. "He knows who killed the noble-woman, Lady Eileen."

It was a statement, not a question, and additional information she hadn't known before—a name.

Greer nodded. "Aye, I believe that's why he's been placed in the dungeon. The guard I spoke to said that the earl had finally made a decision on what to do with Mac this afternoon."

The corners of Drake's mouth flinched.

Unease prickled down her back. "What is it?"

"Ye've been honest with me. Now I need to do the same with ye." Several heavy steps passed by the door, and they both ducked into the shadows. When nothing came of it, he continued in a whisper, "The real reason I've been sent here, and what hinges on me becoming a knight, is discovering how she died. Lady Eileen's da, Lord Androll, doesna believe her death was an accident and suspects foul play. I've been ordered to uncover who wanted her dead."

"And ye've been asking questions today," Greer surmised.

"I thought I was subtle." Drake lifted a shoulder casually. "I've no' ever had to find a killer before. I'm a warrior, no' a constable."

"Lord Calver must know ye're looking for him." The tension that had bled from Greer's shoulders knotted back up once more. "If he does and ye go down to the dungeon right now, they're no' going to be honest with ye, Drake. Lord Calver wants

Mac dead so his secrets are buried along with Lady Eileen and my brother."

A muscle worked in Drake's jaw. "Ye're right. Give me a moment to think. We need a plan."

"We do," she agreed. "But no' an honest one."

Drake cocked his head, his immediate distaste for her suggestion apparent before she could even divulge her idea.

"Arrest me." She put her wrists out in supplication. "Take me to the dungeon with a dagger hidden in my skirts."

"And how will ye escape with only a dagger?"

"Tell the guards they can do what they want with me."

He balked in horror.

"As soon as they open the cell door, I'll attack them, but so will ye," she continued. "Then we can free Mac and make our way through the castle with ye leading the way to ensure the path is clear. We travel to the king with Mac and have him bear witness as to what happened that day. By the time Lord Calver can dream of catching us, he will be the one in the snare, no' us."

"I dinna like it," he said through gritted teeth.

"Do ye have a better idea that is more honorable?" She folded her arms over her chest.

His gaze focused on the back wall for a moment, his brow furrowed in concentration. "Nay."

"Can ye lie?" she asked.

He smirked. "No' convincingly."

"Ye'll need to." She stretched a hand toward him. "For me."

He enveloped her in his arms once more, tender in a way that made her want to sigh and rest her head against his powerful chest. "I dinna want ye to get hurt."

"I willna get hurt," she promised. "This is the only chance for us to save him. Otherwise, tomorrow morning..."

Drake nodded in solemn understanding.

Tomorrow morning would be too late. They had only this one night to succeed, or Mac would be put to death.

❧ 18 ❧

The plan to get into the dungeon did not sit well with Drake. Not at all. Especially the bit about telling the men to have their way with Greer once she was in the cell.

These men thought he was there to aid them, not deceive them. Not harm them.

He bound the rope loosely about Greer's wrists, enough that it would appear secure, but she could easily slip free.

"I dinna want to do this," he said again.

"We dinna have a choice." Her eyes filled with such desperation, he could not help but hold her close one final time, as though that might somehow keep her safe.

There was another aspect to their scheme they had not discussed. Failure. That if they were caught, they both could be put to death the following morning with Mac.

Though Drake did not wish to say it out loud, he could not stop his mind from probing at the possibility. With battle came the risk of death.

And they were preparing to walk into a great battle.

Greer looked up at him when he released her. "Ye're the only person I've ever trusted in this way," she said softly. "I...ye...I've no' ever felt this way..." She shook her head, offering a mirthless laugh instead of the completion of her statement. "We need to go, aye?"

But what she was afraid to say, Drake was not. He had never told Anice how he felt when he believed he had lost his heart to her. Now he realized that the tenderness he had experienced then was nothing in comparison to how Greer made his chest squeeze with emotion.

If this were the only time that he could ever tell her, he would do so with his whole heart while he still had it to give. He cradled her face between his hands, caressing the smoothness of her skin. "I love ye, Greer."

She sucked in a breath, but he didn't allow her a chance to protest his words or offer a self-deprecating remark. Instead, he gently pulled her toward the door to the laundry, leading her toward the dungeon—and hoped to God her plan would work.

This time, he lit the sconce before he descended the stairs and made considerable noise so the guards would know of his arrival.

"Oy!" someone called. "Who goes there?"

Drake glanced one last time beside him at Greer, where she was tethered to him by the rope. Her expression was filled with all the love she had not confessed to him, as he had done to her. Not that an admission was necessary between them when it was so very apparent.

He would do anything for this woman. And he was about to prove it.

"'Tis Drake," he called out as he strode through the open area at the bottom of the stairs.

Greer's expression slid from love to hate as she fell into her role. "Let go of me, ye cur." Her lip curled in disgust.

Drake envied her ability to change her skin so easily, to glide so effortlessly into a role. He'd always been honest to a fault, sometimes losing jobs and friends because of it.

Much like what Bean was experiencing.

"I found her prowling through the castle." Drake nodded to Greer. It wasn't a lie—he had found her prowling around the castle—and so it was said without guilt.

The guard unlocked the door and let it groan open but did not step back to allow them passage. "Hand her over."

"I can bring her in," Drake offered.

"'Tis no' necessary," the guard replied.

Drake was not so readily put off. "I've no' seen this part of the castle yet. Now is as good a time as any, eh?"

The man folded his arms over his chest.

"Am I no' here to train ye?" Drake asked, his ire rising along-side his desperation. "Out of my way, man."

The guard shook his head. "Ye're not to come into the dungeon, on the earl's orders."

"The king sent me at the earl's request," Drake said, lacing his voice with authority.

The man hesitated.

Greer tugged at the ropes. "Let me go. I've no' done anything wrong."

Her pleading came across as too genuine, the pitch to her voice indicative of real fear. Drake turned to look at her.

"Please," she said.

It was so easy to recall when she'd last whispered that word to him—when they lay in bed with one another, their bodies alight with desire.

"Let me go." Her eyes were wide, and she pulled at the ropes.

Drake had tied them loose to help her free herself later. Apparently, they were too loose, and easily fell off from her hands with the slight tug.

There was a single moment where everyone froze as the rope fell soundlessly to the ground. Greer was the first to recover, not running from the dungeon but toward it, charging at the guard like an enraged bull.

It was an unexpected turn of events, but one Drake would not leave her to fight on her own. He raced forward, grabbed the iron door and shoved it hard into the man.

The guard's head hit the wall as he was shoved backward, and he slumped to the ground.

Perfect.

Drake would avoid causing any permanent harm to the Lochmaben guards if possible.

Greer immediately knelt at the man's side and slipped the key ring from his belt. "Now we find Mac."

But before they could push deeper into the dark hall of cells, the sound of rushing footsteps and rattling chainmail told Drake their initial attack had been noticed.

He put himself in front of Greer. "Stay behind me, aye?"

She nodded. He slid free his sword and squared his body in front of the woman he loved, striding toward the men as they rushed at him. He kept his steps quick so Greer could inspect as many of the cells as possible. If Mac was in there, Drake needed only to cause a distraction for a short time while she freed him.

But as the men raced at him with apparent determination to fight, unease shifted inside him. He did not want to fight them, to harm, or possible kill them. These were to be his brothers in arms, many of them scarcely even old enough to be called men.

"Stop," Drake bellowed at them.

Much to his surprise, they stopped, their confusion evident at whether to follow the man sent by the king or the orders of their earl.

"There's a wee lad locked in this dungeon," Drake said, implementing the opportunity for honesty in an effort to appeal to their morality. "He's been unjustly accused and shouldna ever have been thrown down here. If we dinna free him now, he will be hanged tomorrow."

A guilty look crossed some men's faces. They knew.

And Drake would appeal to that.

"Today, this lad is a stranger to ye," Drake said. "But in the future, mayhap it will be someone ye know. A nephew, a brother, a son."

A sharp gasp sounded behind him, followed by a choked cry. He glanced to his right, through a barred window where a boy was curled in the corner of a cell, looking more dead than alive.

At once, Drake's heart flinched at the state of the lad, even as victory surged through his veins.

They had found Mac.

THE PILE OF FILTHY RAGS HUDDLED IN THE CORNER DIDN'T look human. Except Greer could see the skinny arms curled around the bent knees, far too small to be that of a man.

Mac.

A cry erupted from her, the pain within her chest too exquisite to bear.

She fumbled with the keys. Her nerves, which had always been steady at the most crucial times, were now tremulous with the knowledge of what she might lose if she did not get the key in the lock.

Pulse racing, she jabbed at the hole with the bit of metal, missing three times before the shank clattered inside and the mechanism within gave with a click.

"I dinna want to fight ye," Drake said behind her to the soldiers.

She didn't bother to throw a glance over her shoulder, not when all her focus had to remain on Mac. There was a damp, earthy scent throughout the dungeon, with an underlying fetid odor permeating the cells.

"Mac," she said softly.

The pile groaned.

"My sweet boy." Her voice caught as she went to him and pulled him into her arms.

He'd lost weight, and his cheeks had gone hollow in a face that was once full of good health. His warm brown eyes found hers and filled with tears.

"Ye're no' real," he whispered as a tear slid down his cheek, washing a trail of grime from his skin.

"I am," Greer said in a cracked voice.

"I canna believe ye're real," he said. "For if ye're no', it will break my heart."

"I'm real," Greer said in a firm voice and pressed a kiss to his sweaty forehead. With that, she stood up, bringing him with her. "We're taking ye away from here. To safety. Can ye walk?"

Mac's scant weight leaned against her, but he remained standing as they strode forward together. "Aye, I can walk." His feet were bare atop the gray rushes, his skin smeared with dirt.

Anger pushed up in Greer, but she had to swallow it down. Now was not the time for allowing her emotions to overwhelm her. She needed to focus on removing him to safety, where he could never be hurt like this again.

"I'm stronger than ye," Drake said outside the cell. The guards watched him warily and maintained an arm's length distance between them.

"I'm faster than ye," Drake continued as he took a step closer to them. They all took a step back. "And I'm better trained. What is being done here is wrong. This lad is still a bairn. He shouldna ever have been here from the start, and each of ye knows that. I dinna want to hurt ye as I'm doing what is right, but I will if needs must."

Greer led Mac from the dungeon cell and down the corridor to where the barred door stood open. The man that had been knocked unconscious was now missing. Mayhap nearby.

It was hard not to run when her muscles were firing with unnatural energy. But already, Mac wheezed with the effort.

She winced at the pathetic sound. Mac had always been a child of limitless energy, running fast as a deer through the meadow, leaping like a rabbit over fallen trees and other objects. Now he seemed an old man with joints gone stiff with age.

As they neared the open door, he began to pick up speed, and Greer matched his pace. A glance behind her confirmed Drake remained with the guards, speaking to them. She couldn't hear him over the huff of Mac's labored breathing, but there was a ring of authority to his voice. Whatever he said held the men at bay.

A moment of unease flickered through her. Had Drake meant to follow them or stay behind? She could figure out where to flee to and what to do to keep Mac safe, of course. But she hadn't bid farewell to Drake.

I love ye, Greer.

Pain laced through her.

He was saying farewell then. She knew that now.

Mac stumbled slightly, and Greer caught him, managing to hold his slight body upright. His skin was burning as hot as the sun beneath her hands. No wonder he was so weak and tired. He was terribly ill.

"We have to go up these stairs." As she said it, Greer noted Mac's gaze swept up the steep stone staircase with a fearful look.

But Mac did not protest. His stick-thin legs pumped their way upward. Never once did he slow, even as his breathing became a panting wheeze.

They were almost to the landing when a figure appeared behind them, too silent for Greer to have heard in their approach. Too fast. She spun about in surprise, but she knew she would be too late to protect Mac.

Except no protection was needed. Drake gave her a nod and scooped her brother into his arms. Below them, one of the guards closed the gate once more and locked it. With the exception of the man Drake had struck by the gate, no one had been hurt.

Incredible.

Drake had managed to appeal to the morality of the men despite Greer thinking the only way could be through deception. Not that there was time to think on that now. Already he was rushing out into the hall, turning his head from side to side to ensure all was clear before darting out.

Greer caught up with him, shadowing his every move as they rushed into the entryway of the castle. So close to freedom.

"Where do ye think ye're going?" A knife flew through the air and sparked off the stone wall a mere inch in front of Drake's face. He stopped abruptly and spun around to face Lord Calver, who stood in a loose tunic, his hair wild from sleep. A guard stood at his side, one whose offended rub at the back of his head indicated he was the one Drake had struck in the dungeon. No doubt he'd fled to notify Lord Calver.

Drake rounded on the old earl, his face hard with rage. "Ye've kept this lad under lock and key for no justified reason—"

"Arrest him," the earl shouted, his face florid.

The guard hesitated.

Drake gently set Mac to his feet and nudged him in Greer's direction. She ran to her little brother before he could get to her and wrapped her arms protectively around him, drawing him back.

"I've been sent here by order of the king," Drake said with full confidence. "If ye arrest me, ye are defying his orders."

"He wanted ye to train my men," Lord Calver gave a derisive snort and shot a vicious glare to the guard who had not acted on his command. "To train these inept guards. How is arresting ye for releasing my prisoner defying his orders? It will take but a word from me. How ye turned on me, and I had no choice but to toss ye in the dungeon."

Mac shivered in Greer's arms. She could not see the castle entrance from where she stood to determine if more guards were lying in wait there, nor what awaited her beyond. The earl could have had the portcullis thrown down, trapping them in the castle, making them run like rabbits until they were finally caught.

"That isna why I'm here." Drake lifted his chin. "I'm here to bring Lady Eileen's killer to justice."

Lord Calver's hands clenched at his sides.

"Her neck wasna broken from a fall," Drake said. "And I have a witness to prove it."

"The woman in the field," Mac whispered. "'Twas him," he said, his voice stronger. "'Twas the earl who did it."

The earl's face went from red to white.

"Arrest him," he sputtered.

The guard at his side did not move.

"They were fighting." Mac withdrew from Greer's arms and stood on his own, even as she tried to pull him back.

But Mac pushed away from her, his tone unwavering as he pointed to the earl, as though the story of a woman's unjust death and his incarceration sent energy pumping through his veins. "The lady said he was stealing money from the king."

"Silence," Lord Calver bellowed.

But Mac would not be silenced and continued, his voice ringing off the stonework, "She said she'd tell, and he lunged at her, attacking her before shoving her down the hill."

"I should have killed ye when I had the chance," the earl cried in outrage as he grabbed a sword and dagger from the guard at his side and raced toward Mac.

❧ 19 ❧

Drake lunged in front of the earl as the man threw the dagger toward Mac and Greer, followed immediately by a vicious swing of the sword. There was only enough time to see Greer curling her body around her brother before Drake obstructed Lord Calver's wild assault.

Their swords connected with a clash that rang sharply off the stone walls. "Get him out of here," Drake growled to Greer through gritted teeth.

Movement sounded behind him—what he could only assume was Greer doing as he asked. He needed them gone. Safe.

Even if it meant he didn't know where she went. Or how he might find her again someday.

Or that this might be the last time he ever saw her.

He didn't regret his decision to tell her he loved her, and now, more than ever, he was especially glad to have made the admission.

Lord Calver swung his blade once more, and again Drake impeded the blow. He couldn't retaliate against an earl. No warrior could attack a nobleman and live to tell the tale.

Even if the man was a murderer.

"Dinna just stand there," Lord Calver hissed at the guard. "If ye dinna summon help, I'll have ye hanged for yer betrayal."

The man sprinted off, this time to follow orders at the threat of his own neck.

Calver returned his attention to Drake, his eyes bulging and bloodshot with rage. "Get out of my way."

Drake remained where he stood, blocking the earl's path to where Greer and Mac had run. "The lad goes free. He hasna done anything wrong."

"The lad knows too bloody much." The earl's lip curled. "I'll have ye killed if ye dinna move." He jabbed at Drake with his blade, the effort careless with a lack of finesse.

Drake shifted back slightly to avoid the strike. "I dinna want to fight ye."

"Of course, ye dinna want to fight me." The nobleman whipped his blade at Drake's chest. "I'm an earl. And ye're no' even a knight. It was an insult for the king to send someone so common."

Men's shouts sounded in the distance.

"I'll kill ye myself." Calver thrust his blade toward Drake, who leapt to avoid being skewered.

A wall hit his heels.

The earl grinned and charged at him a final time. Drake darted to the left. As he did so, he lowered his sword to keep from hitting the lord. Except that the earl had moved more swiftly than Drake had anticipated. Mayhap it was that his da's blade, with its razored edge, was exceptionally sharp after the additional honing at the blacksmith's, or mayhap it was the way the man dove at him. Regardless of the cause, the man brushed the tip of the sword point, which sliced through the earl's tunic as if it were made of air. Blood welled against the light-colored fabric of his night clothes.

The crimson stain spread far too quickly to be simply a normal wound. Drake was immediately reminded of an injury he saw on the battlefield once, where a warrior's thigh was cut in battle, and his blood gushed out too rapidly to be staunched. The man had died within minutes.

The soldiers rounded the corner as the earl sank to his knees in a glistening puddle of blood widening around him.

"He stabbed me," Lord Calver whispered in a hoarse, frightened voice. "He stabbed me."

The guard who had gone for help rushed to him and crouched at his side. He drew up the hem of the tunic where gore spurted from the wound.

Lord Calver's face had gone pale, and his eyes rolled up into his head.

Drake stood there as the man fell backward, his head hitting the stone floor with a sickening thud, the pain never felt by the earl, who was already dead.

"He's killed the earl," one of the guards shouted.

"My blade nicked him," Drake said in disbelief.

"Does this look like a nick to ye?" the man kneeling at the earl's side demanded.

"I dinna want to fight him," Drake said with force. "He wouldna leave me be."

"Arrest him," another guard said to the others. "Lady Calver will decide what to do with ye."

Drake almost groaned, certain how Lady Calver would treat him after he had rejected her.

The men advanced toward him as one. Men who had been willing to allow a lad to go free were not so amenable when their lord had been slain. No matter how cruel he might be.

But Drake would not run. He was no coward. He had done what he knew to be right. First, by protecting the boy who had been unjustly locked in the dungeon. Then by refusing to fight the earl.

Still, somehow, it had all gone horribly wrong. In the end,

Drake would put his faith in justice, which he knew would prevail in the end. It always did.

One of the guards pulled his hands behind his back.

"I've got him," another smaller guard said in a testy, gruff voice from beneath a helm.

The shackles that went around his wrists were far looser than he had anticipated. But the guard behind him did not tighten them further. Instead, he shoved Drake forward to follow the other guard leading the way back to the dungeon.

It was the same path he had taken earlier, except Drake would not be rescuing someone this time. He would be thrown down there himself, locked in a cell to await his sentence.

He squared his shoulders and lifted his chin, ready to face whatever came his way.

They turned down the corridor in the direction of the dungeon stairs while the commotion of the earl's death was marked with shouts of alarm and the high-pitched cry of Lady Calver.

All at once, the guard behind Drake rushed past him and threw a punch at the guard in the front. The man slid to the ground like a grain sack and the smaller guard with the helm grabbed his arm, tugging him toward a side door.

The guard tilted their face upward, and familiar green eyes sparkled back at him. "Bean is waiting out front with Mac. Let us make haste before the guards come for us."

Then, before he could even regain his thoughts, Greer shoved him toward the door, and together they began to run.

SWEAT PRICKLED ON GREER'S BROW AS THEY RAN. BENEATH THE heavy guard's attire, all of her was slick with perspiration that burned as it dripped into the slight cut from where the earl's dagger had grazed her ribs.

Bean was outside where he said he'd be, with Drake's horse affixed to a wagon with Mac hidden beneath a cloth.

"Get underneath," Greer ordered.

Drake hesitated at this, but she nudged him. "If ye're caught, we all are. It will be easier to flee if ye are concealed."

That seemed to make up his mind as he quickly and silently disappeared under the canvas. Greer climbed up onto the narrow seat of the cart beside Bean.

"Where's Brevis?" She asked of his horse.

Bean clicked his tongue, and the destrier trotted forward. "Bringing him would be too obvious. I'll get him back when this business is sorted out." He said it with a determined tone, but she could make out the hurt brimming in his blue eyes.

"Ye're a good lad." She ruffled his hair and was rewarded with a sad smile.

The cart rattled over the lowered drawbridge as they left the castle. Still, the tension didn't ease from Greer's shoulders, not even when they had passed through the raised portcullis and out into the village. The shuttered wooden gate came into view, and that was when her heart slipped into her throat, its beat echoing back at her from her side as the wound made its presence known.

Two guards stood out front, one with his head leaned back, clearly sleeping while the other looked their way.

"Gate's closed," the alert one said.

The other snorted awake. "Closed," he reiterated in a thick voice.

"Aye, I see that, and ye need to open it," Greer said in a husky voice meant to make her sound more like a man.

"Nay," the first one scoffed.

"I take it ye dinna get the orders this afternoon?" Greer demanded. "I knew it. I hope that warrior from the king can get this lot into shape." With an exaggerated sigh, she continued, speaking as though they were dullards who needed her to drag her words to be understood. "The earl needs this cloth dyed by midmorning. It canna be done in time if we wait for the bloody gates to finally open at dawn."

The men looked at one another.

"Ye can go ask him if ye like." Greer gestured back to the castle. "I'm sure he'll no' mind being woken in the middle of the night for a task he ordered done this morn."

The guards didn't bother to reply and instead set to work, pulling the bar free from the massive gates, and drawing one side open wide enough for the cart to pass through.

Bean's hands were white knuckled where he gripped the reins of the horse, and his skin appeared to be made of wax in the glow of the moonlight. But he kept the slight click of his tongue normal enough to pass without arousing suspicion.

"Fine horse," one of the men said as they drove by.

"An old one that'll be dead soon," Greer muttered. "Ye think they'd lend a healthy destrier for a bit of cloth to be dyed?" She scoffed. "Close up the damn gates before someone slips through who shouldna."

They didn't question her as the cart cleared the massive gate, and it slowly shut behind her. The hollow thud of the bar falling into place thundered behind them.

Only then did Greer finally exhale a shaky breath.

"Ye lied," Bean said. "A lot."

"I did," she agreed quietly, grateful to drop the husky, masculine voice that strained at her throat. "And I'd do it all again to save my brother and Drake."

Bean glanced up at her and nodded. "I would too."

"Ye did well, lad." She smiled at him. "Verra well."

The helm cocooned heat all around her head and stank of wet metal, but she kept it in place as they rode to avoid drawing notice. She directed Bean to the small cottage where she and Mac lived, set near the water for her washing and away from most of the other villagers.

Once they stopped, she rushed into her house for clean

clothes for her and Mac. The familiar scent of fresh-cut wood from the table they had painstakingly built together, and the residual smoky peat scent from their fire carried with it the smell of home, of comfort. Tears pricked her eyes for the life they had lost. But she had no time to waste on sentiment.

She tugged off the soldier's garb and hid it in a bundle with some bedding before throwing on a fresh dress. Her movements were swift despite the pain in her rib. A glance confirmed it was little more than a slice. Nothing to worry over.

She grabbed clothes and shoes for Bean, as well as a small vial. The tincture had been concocted by the local healer for a fever Mac had several months before, when he fell ill with the same malady that had stricken many of the village children. It would surely help him now.

Within minutes, she was back in the cart, lying beside Mac under the tarp while Drake took her place on the bench beside Bean, disguised by the cover of darkness. They set off at a swift pace, intent on getting as far from Lochmaben as the night would take them. Greer snuggled her brother close and let him sleep against her as they rode on, reveling in every exhale of his warm breath against her collarbone. They rode on through the night and did not stop until dawn. Even then, they only did so within the woods near a remote village.

Bean was sent to obtain provisions for them as the rest remained behind. Greer squinted up at Drake as he drew back the tarp, exposing the brilliance of the morning light. Greer put her hand over her eyes to block out the rising sun.

Beside her lay Mac, who had begun to wake when the cart drew to a stop. He beamed at Greer now, appearing at least somewhat restored from the water and bread given to him the night before while she was in the cottage.

"How are ye?" Greer asked, sitting upright and stretching from a night of cramped sleep. A pinch at her side reminded her where she'd been caught by the dagger. She quickly lowered her arms and wrapped them around her to keep anyone from seeing her discomfort.

It was a mere scratch, nothing for anyone to lose their head over. Mac's welfare was far more important.

"Ye came for me." Her brother pushed into a sitting position in a slow, pained way that touched deep into her heart.

"Of course I did." She ruffled his hair. It was dirty, aye, but it was still Mac's hair, and she'd take it however she could get it.

She uncorked the tincture. Its sharp scent cut through the air. Mac used to wrinkle his nose at the odor and beg to be left alone. He did not protest now as she brought it to his lips and let two drops fall against his pale tongue.

Once Bean returned with food and drink, Greer helped Mac eat a meat pie and drink a bit of ale. Though the sustenance seemed to fortify him, his eyes once more began to fall closed.

"I'm so verra tired," he murmured as he slid down into the bed of the wagon again.

"Rest." Greer smoothed a hand over his warm brow. It was not burning with the same fire as the night before, and for that, she was grateful.

What he really needed was a cottage where he could take several days to sleep and recover. Mayhap even a sennight or a fortnight. But that wasn't a luxury they had. Not with Lord Calver's soldiers most likely searching for them. While the guards' lack of experience would most likely lead to a haphazard search, Greer would take no chances.

She had lost Mac once. She would not lose him again.

Nor would she allow anything to happen to Bean, who had so bravely aided them. And Drake...

Her gaze settled on his strong profile, and her fingertips ached to trace over the dark hair prickling his jaw, to curl into the cradle of his arms and breathe in his familiar scent. A strange aching sensation filled her chest, but one she now recognized.

She could not lose the only man she had ever loved.

❦ 20 ❧

There were no stops at inns on the journey to Dunfermline Palace, especially with the cart traveling at a slower pace than being on horseback. Though Drake wished nothing more than to provide comfortable beds and hot food for Greer and wee Mac, he knew anywhere they went would expose them. They needed to reach Dunfermline with haste, preferably before Lord Calver's men could, and secure the king's ear first.

Lord Calver still had men who were loyal to him—even in death. The guards had proved that the night Drake fled Lochmaben. Especially with Lady Calver in charge of the men until the earl's heir took his place. No doubt she would seek to protect her financial independence for as long as possible after losing her husband. Further scandal would jeopardize that.

Drake did not want to see Greer, Mac or Bean lose their freedom over this. And so it was that they rested where they could on the trail, in a cave one night, at the edge of a clearing another night. Through it all, Greer remained at Mac's side, vigilant to the point of not caring for herself.

"Dinna forget to eat," Drake cautioned, nudging a bit of cheese and bread her way.

"In a moment," she distractedly replied as she wiped at Mac's face with a damp bit of linen.

"Greer, I'm fine." Mac turned his face to get away from her ministrations. "Ye need to eat. As Drake says."

She paused and lowered her hand. Flecks of sunlight filtered down from the canopy of leaves overhead and shone on her, highlighting how pale her skin had become. Shadows showed under her eyes, and a fine sheen of sweat glistened on her brow.

The day was cool, one that shouldn't warrant any sweat at all. Drake frowned. "Greer—"

"I'm no' hungry." She stepped down from the cart with the linen towel still in her hands. Upon landing, she staggered. While she managed to catch herself, it was enough to worry Drake.

He followed her to the small stream where she sank to her knees and settled on her heels to wash the cloth in the quick flowing stream. They hadn't been alone together since they left Lochmaben. She had put her entire focus on Mac. While Drake understood her reasoning, he could not stifle his alarm over her wellbeing.

"Greer," he said her name gently.

She looked up at him. She appeared so small where she sat, so exhausted that it pulled at him.

"Are ye well?" he knelt in the soft, damp grass and swept a lock of auburn hair from her brow. Her skin was flushed and hot with fever.

He drew his hand back in surprise.

"I just need rest." Greer squeezed the water from the linen and pushed up to her feet.

As she did so, Drake couldn't help but notice she favored her right side. "Are ye hurt?" he demanded.

"I'm no' the one who needs to be helped." She gazed at him with glassy eyes, her cheeks flushed.

How had he not noticed it until now?

"I need to help Mac, and I need to help..." Her voice caught. "I need to help ye, Drake, so ye'll be free from any punishment." She wavered. "I need..."

He reached for her and enfolded her burning body against him, supporting her. "Ye need help, lass."

She shook her head, but even as she did so, her lashes dipped over her cheeks. He lifted her into his arms.

"Nay," she whispered. But her protest was feebly given, and by the time they returned to the cart, her head slumped against his chest.

"Greer." Mac straightened as they approached. "What's happened?"

"She requires a healer," Drake said. "Ye both do. Beathan, stay here, aye? I'll be back."

The nearby village had a healer, a middle-aged woman with a hut on the outskirts nestled into the woods as if she were used to attending people who did not wish to be found. She did not ask questions and took the pouch of coins he offered with quiet gratitude.

The woman needed only a bit of time with Greer before coming out to speak to Drake and handing him a pouch. "If ye keep the wound clean with garlic and honey, the poison will leech from it. The willow bark tea will help bring her fever down. The lad's too." She nodded to where Mac stood anxiously by the door to the cottage.

"Her wound?" Drake asked.

"Aye." The woman traced a line on her side. "Here. A slice from something. Mayhap a dagger."

The dagger Lord Calver had thrown. It had hit Greer, and she had never told him, focusing instead on her brother even as her wound began to fester. Something ice-cold spread over Drake. Fear.

He had seen men who died from insignificant injuries that swiftly reddened with contagion.

"Will she recover?" Drake asked, a tight band squeezing at him.

The healer hesitated. "Just as ye canna guarantee a soldier will survive a battle, I canna guarantee her fever will break. God willing, she will, but I dinna have His divine gift. Only some herbs and the sense to put them to proper use."

Drake nodded in understanding. It was as good an answer as he'd get.

Greer was lying on the table when he entered the one-room cottage. A fire crackled in the middle of the clean space with a pot hung over its center, releasing the damp, earthy scent of herbs into the air. The healer nodded, indicating he was fine to take Greer.

Still, he hesitated. Greer was so still where she lay, her face pale. When he'd fought Lord Calver at Lochmaben, he had presumed she had left and was on her way to safety with Mac; that he would undoubtedly never see her again.

But now that he had her back with him, he was in danger of losing her once more. Forever.

An ache split in his chest. He picked her up as gently as possible and carried her the entire way back to the cart, with Mac anxiously fluttering about by his side.

They didn't have the time to spare for her to get the rest she needed, it was true, but he managed to find a cave set deep in the woods. They would have to give her time to heal, at least until her fever broke. Mayhap a day. Possibly two.

He only hoped it would be enough. While he would have preferred an inn with a warm, comfortable bed, he knew she would not want to risk Mac being caught.

Nor him.

Drake stayed up through the night, watching over her the way she had watched over Mac and prayed that her skin would cool, that he would not lose her.

⚜

THE SNAPPING POPS OF A FIRE ROUSED GREER FROM HER SLEEP. Sweat poured from her body, leaving her kirtle clinging to her legs. She shoved at the heavy blanket covering her, writhing to escape the overwhelming heat.

"Ye're fever is breaking." The voice was masculine and soothing.

A damp cloth pressed to Greer's brow, and she immediately relaxed, relishing the coolness.

Something nagged at the back of her mind—anxiety, a fear of some kind.

Her eyes flew open. "Mac."

Drake put a hand to her shoulder. "He's here." He nodded toward two bundles on the other side of the fire. "Sleeping next to Beathan," he added quietly.

"Is he well?" Greer asked, her throat raspy with dryness.

"Verra well." He chuckled.

"Mac is recovered?" Panic rose in her chest, and she recalled how ill he had still been when last she saw him.

"Aye. He and Beathan were playing so loudly earlier that I feared they might give away our location."

Their location?

Only then did Greer pay attention to her surroundings. The stone walls, the dirt floor, the cart tucked in front of them like a barrier and Drake's horse barely visible near the mouth of the cave just beyond.

She rose onto her elbows. "Where are we?"

"A cave somewhere in the woods on the outskirts of a village so small, I dinna think it has a name." He ran the back of his fingers over her cheek.

She caught Drake's hand and held it. "How long have we been here?"

"Two days. This is our third night. There was a point..." He paused and gazed at her with a pained expression. "I dinna think yer fever would ever break."

"Three nights?" she gasped. "We canna afford three nights."

Her illness had doubled the time of the journey. Lord Calver's guards would arrive at Dunfermline Palace first. The king would hear a plea on behalf of Lord and Lady Calver before any other explanation could be given.

"Nor can we afford to lose ye," Drake said gently.

She shook her head. "Nay. Saving Mac, keeping him safe, proving his innocence and yers. That is what matters."

Drake lightly squeezed her hand. "Saving ye mattered to us all too."

She continued to shake her head. She wasn't important. There was nothing to her but the constant struggle to survive, one with endless days of wet laundry, where stealing sometimes was all that got them by. The time spent on her recovery was too precious and pointlessly wasted.

"We need to leave now." She pulled her hand from his. "Tonight."

A band around her ribs tightened as she flexed her abdomen to rise. It was then she realized she wore an overlarge tunic over her torso with the top of her kirtle pushed down around her waist. She glanced up at Drake.

He shrugged. "It was easier to change yer dressing, which we will need to do now anyway." He hesitated. "If I may."

"There's no time," she hissed.

"We'll leave in the morning." His tone brokered no room for argument.

But she was never one who abided being told what to do. "Now."

Drake glanced over his shoulder to the sleeping boys. "They

need rest. As do I. Another few hours will make a difference to all of us. But it willna make a difference..."

His words tapered off.

"To those who await us," she finished for him.

Drake's mouth thinned in response, and he guided a mug into her hands. "All will be well."

Fear and doubt pressed in on her with certainty as she stared at the murky liquid within. "It willna be well. It never is for those who are no' born into nobility."

"It will." A muscle worked in his jaw. "Let me change yer bandage, aye?" He motioned for her to drink.

She did, swallowing down the musty concoction before handing the mug back and lying down for him to see to her wound. He turned his gaze away in apparent consideration of her modesty as she eased up the tunic. She gave a little chuckle. "Ye've seen it all anyway." Even still, her cheeks went hot with a fierce blush.

Slowly, his stare returned to her, and he set to work. His large hands were tender as he worked, the same as they were when he loved her. And though his efforts were not sensual in nature, her body reacted as if they were.

His fingertips whispered over her skin and left a ripple of gooseflesh tingling over her body. Heat gathered between her thighs and made her nipples tighten into hard peaks beneath the thin tunic.

He felt it too. At one point, he glanced back at the sleeping lads with a hint of disappointment at their presence.

It was thrilling to be touched so. At least until he smeared an awful-smelling, sticky substance on the wound that made it sting.

"Garlic and honey to draw the poison of yer wound out." He said it with the practiced air of a healer, no doubt repeating what he had been told.

His obvious attempt to reassure her brought an endearing smile to her lips for this man who had cared for her as no other had ever bothered to do. She sat up as he wound fresh linen about her ribs, and their eyes locked as he did so.

"I meant what I said to ye, back at Lochmaben." He tucked the linen against itself, secured into place by the light tension.

His eyes were inky pools of darkness, and she drank them in, letting herself sink so deeply, she fancied she brushed his soul. "Ye said a lot of things at Lochmaben," she murmured.

The corner of his lip lifted in a boyish grin that made her want to kiss him again and again until the need to cradle his body between her thighs overwhelmed her.

"I did." He leaned over her, and her pulse ticked faster in anticipation.

But he didn't kiss her. Instead, he swept her hair back and delicately cradled her jaw. The caress was so pleasant that she closed her eyes against it.

Weariness swept over her and made her not want to open her eyes again. Her body grew lax, and her lids were suddenly very heavy.

"I love ye." His thumb brushed over her cheek. "Ye've made my heart whole again."

Warm tears prickled in her eyes, for he made her heart whole too. And that was saying something when she had spent the better part of her life with it in tattered shreds.

She wanted to tell him what he meant to her as well, but her tongue felt thick in her mouth, and her eyelids seemed to weigh far too much to lift them. He drew her into the embrace of his arms.

"Sleep, my love." His voice was like black velvet, gliding over her and pulling her into the quiet heat of slumber.

But before she finally succumbed, she could not help but wonder what the next day might bring. And what awaited them at Dunfermline Palace.

21

The next morning, Drake awoke by first light. The lads still slumbered, which was fortunate, as it kept them from seeing how Drake had held Greer in his arms as they slept.

But he would not have let her go for anything. With her skin against his, at least he would be able to discern if her fever returned. Thankfully, she had remained cool all night, her breath soft and even where it fanned against his chest.

He withdrew his arms from around her, and she blinked her eyes open.

"How are ye feeling?" he asked.

Her brow furrowed. "Concerned." She reached up for his face, touching her palm to his cheek in a caress he savored. "We shouldna have wasted so much time."

"Greer?" A sleepy voice asked.

Drake regretfully pulled away, not wanting the lads to see them together.

"Greer," Mac exclaimed as he bounded from his makeshift bed and ran over to her. "Are ye well?"

"Aye." She laughed and shared a grin with Drake over her brother's enthusiasm.

"We were worried about ye, but Drake said ye'd be fine," Bean said.

"It takes more than a fever to keep me down." Greer rose from her bedroll and tousled Bean's hair.

Drake noticed she no longer favored her right side as she had before. She truly was feeling better. He breathed a sigh of relief. But it was short-lived as her words came back to him. She was concerned about their arrival into Dunfermline.

And she had every right to be.

Drake was concerned himself.

The worry did not abate as they broke their fast and prepared the cart for their journey. There were many ways their arrival into Dunfermline could be received, but most likely, it would not be with a welcome reception.

Likewise, there were many ways the king might react. But after inadvertently killing one of the crown's most lucrative supporters, Drake anticipated his future to be bleak.

Prison, if he were lucky, but most likely, he would hang.

Certainly, any dreams of becoming a knight would never be realized. He'd be fortunate to escape with his life.

His gaze followed Greer as she moved about the cave, helping to pack their meager belongings. Though she smiled and jested with the lads, her concern was evident in the tension around her lips and the slight crease across her forehead.

Suddenly, a chilling thought jarred him.

They had coupled together. He had taken her maidenhead. A woman without experience would not know how to keep a babe from her womb. If he were to die, he would leave her with a bairn and no support.

She jostled him as she passed by. "Dinna look so serious." Though she said it playfully, he could see the warning in her eyes to keep the blatant unease from his face for the sake of the younger two.

"Let me set up a pallet for ye in the cart." Drake took the bedding from her.

"Ach, I couldna possibly lay down any longer." She waved him off. "I'd like to sit on the bench for a while if that's fine with ye."

"Aye, I'd enjoy the company." His heartbeat quickened. This would be the perfect opportunity to talk to her and convince her that they would have to marry before they arrived in Dunfermline.

For her sake. For the possibility of a bairn.

And because he loved her.

She gave him a genuine smile. "There's something I want to speak with ye on."

"I have something to say as well," he replied.

Within minutes, the cart was secured to Drake's destrier, and the boys settled in the back. They chattered like magpies and tossed hay at one another amid shared laughter. In truth, it was good to see them without thought to what lay in wait at the palace.

"Before we enter Dunfermline, we need to make a stop and assume disguises." Greer nodded to herself, having already agreed in her mind to this ploy.

"Disguises?" Drake asked.

"Aye, so we can sneak into the palace and gain an audience with the king before ye can be arrested."

Drake shook his head. "That is for ye and the lads to do, but no' me."

"Drake." She gazed up at him, her eyes wide with fear. "They'll capture ye."

"I'm a warrior, Greer." He squared his shoulders with the finality of his decision. "I'll no' run or hide."

Those lovely green eyes filled with tears. "They could kill ye."

"And that is what I wished to speak with ye about." He looked away, unable to witness the terror and hurt in her stare. "If I am to die…" he glanced behind them to ensure the lads were not listening and lowered his voice. "What if ye are with child, Greer?"

She scoffed. "I dinna think I am."

"But if ye are. And if I'm gone." Pain resonated through him at the very thought. "I want to ensure ye'll be cared for. I want to give ye my name so that whatever wealth not taken by the king will go to ye, and so that our child wouldna be born a bastard. Ye could go to Skye—"

"Ye're no' going to die."

Drake turned his focus back to her and found her jaw locked tight.

"Dinna even say it," she warned.

"I was serious when I told ye I wanted to marry ye." He put his hand over hers. "No' because of the possibility of a bairn, but because I love ye. I hope to God the king sees fit to allow me to live so that we might continue in life together. But if I am to die—"

"Dinna say that again." She stared down at their hands in her lap. "I'm no' worthy of ye, Drake. I'm a peasant, a thief. A no one."

He gently caressed the back of her hand with his thumb. "Ye were a mother when there was none for yer brother. Ye're a savior, no' only of Mac, but me too."

"Ye're an honorable man." Her voice trembled.

"I've no' always been and may well die a criminal." He drew in a deep breath at the reality looming over him. "But even if things were different—if I were receiving my knighthood and no' being judged—ye are the only one I'd want by my side. A lass as bonny as she is honorable."

She gave a short laugh. "Ye'd be the only person to describe me as such."

"Ye've only stolen to put food in yer bellies and to save Mac.

That doesna make ye a criminal. It makes ye noble." He ran his thumb down her palm where the chapped skin had healed, leaving her skin pink. "When given a choice, ye worked hard for yer living and would have continued to do so were ye no' at the mercy of yer circumstances." He lifted his hand and gently tilted her face up at him. "'Tis for that reason and so many more that I love ye and that I want ye to be my wife."

She pulled in a soft breath but said nothing.

"Will ye?" he asked. "Be my wife?"

GREER COULD SCARCELY BREATHE AROUND THE KNOT IN HER throat, let alone reply. She stared up at Drake, amazed at how he saw better of her than she deserved.

"Aye," she said, finally able to speak again. "Aye, I'll marry ye."

"Ye're going to be married?" Mac squealed excitedly from behind them.

A laugh erupted from Greer, free and giddy with immeasurable joy.

"When?" Bean asked as he scooted closer to them.

"Tonight," Drake said. "And we'll stay at an inn to celebrate."

An icy chill of fear gripped Greer. "'Tis no' safe."

Drake shrugged. "They're already at Dunfermline Palace if they're anywhere. One night." His warm hand atop hers squeezed lightly.

One night together. Most likely, their last.

Greer nodded and managed to keep the catch from her voice as she agreed, "Tonight."

They rode on through the afternoon and arrived at a small kirk outside a village as dusk began to mute the brilliance of the sun. Drake pulled the cart to a stop, and Greer's heart tripped over itself.

"Will here suit ye?" he asked, his hand extended, palm up to her.

She didn't even look at the building, too preoccupied with the handsome man who had captured her wayward heart. The kirk could be a hole in the earth for all she cared. "Aye."

He hopped down from his seat as the boys leapt from the cart and helped her to the ground. The wound at her side no longer pained her, as was evidenced by the lack of discomfort upon landing. Thanks be to God. She did not want to think of her injury and what it had cost them.

What they might still have to sacrifice.

"I want this night with ye," she admitted softly. "I'm glad we are stopping at an inn." She slid her hand into his. "To be alone."

Drake swallowed. "Yer side..."

She shook her head to allay his fears, and together they made their way into the stone building. The priest within agreed to marry them, so as the moon took the place of the sun, Greer and Drake were wed with Bean and Mac as witnesses.

She wished she'd had more than a homespun cloth kirtle to wear, or had thought to pick a few flowers for her hair. But at the end of it all, what she cared about most was the man she was marrying and having her brother and Bean there with them.

Drake watched her through the ceremony with pride shining in his dark eyes, and when he was given permission to kiss his new wife, he leaned forward and gifted her with the sweetest, tenderest kiss any soul had ever tasted.

They located an inn within the town and secured two rooms, one for the lads and one for themselves, for a last night alone together.

Drake led her immediately upstairs and drew her into his arms as soon as the door closed behind them. Their mouths found each other, their tongues stroking. This time it was Drake who untied the leather knot of her kirtle, unthreading the lacing, and pulling her clothing from her body.

She was not at all shy to be in front of him now as she was before, knowing only desire and the need to be as close to him as possible for as long as she could. They didn't rush any part of their joining, taking the time to enjoy one another, teasing with tongues, nipping with gentle teeth, kissing, and loving in every way they could.

When at last they came together, their hands were interlocked, their gazes fixed on one another as Drake's hardness pressed into her. She curled her legs around his waist to lock him against her, undulating with his measured pace.

They watched the pleasure play out over one another's faces as they cherished the slow, sensual connection of their bodies, hearts, and souls. As a flush warmed over Drake's cheeks, Greer felt her own need intensify, pushing them together faster with friction that built in that now-familiar place at her core.

Drake's hands tightened over Greer's as they joined as one with panting breath and sighing moans until, at last, he gave one great, final thrust that sealed them completely. As her release shuddered through her, the telltale swell of him within her let her know he had climaxed at the same time.

The sensation of it was beautiful and wonderful. They clung to one another as their bodies rode over the lapping waves of bliss together until, at last, they drifted back to the awareness of the small bed at the inn, which they lay upon.

There they continued to embrace, each one reluctant to let go. Finally, he withdrew from her and lay at her side, one finger stroking up and down her arm

"I dinna want ye to go tomorrow." Greer lifted her head. "We could slip away tonight with the lads. Go to another part of Scotland where no one need know where we are. Who we are."

His brows flexed as though he was in pain at the very thought. "I canna do that."

"Yer mum and yer sisters," Greer said in chastisement of herself for having selfishly not thought of them.

Drake cupped her face and kissed her. "Forgive me, my love."

"I dinna want tomorrow to come." Her voice broke as she tried to hold back her tears.

He pulled her against him and wrapped his arms around her. Cocooned by his strength, she allowed herself to break. The tears began to fall then, for the love they had only begun to realize and the time together that had been too ephemeral and for the very real possibility that they would be forever wrenched apart.

She cried until her tears ran dry, and then she stayed in his arms longer still, enjoying those precious moments with him. At some point, she finally gave way to the fatigue of her still-healing body, the wonderful relaxation remaining after their shared climax, and the exhaustion of her released emotions.

She fell into a deep sleep in the comfort of his arms and awoke to the light of a new day spilling into the small, rented room. Immediately unease churned in her stomach. She turned to Drake and found him still sleeping, his face relaxed in slumber.

In that quiet, peaceful moment, she studied his face and memorized every detail. How his dark lashes feathered over his high cheekbones, how the slight creases showed at the corners of his eyes even when he wasn't smiling, the way the warm, masculine smell of him made her heart expand in her chest.

As much as she had not wanted the morning to arrive, it had, and the events would be faced together, side by side. She steeled herself for the battle she knew was coming and, for the first time in her life, wondered if she would be strong enough.

❦ 22 ❧

Drake wished they could flee to somewhere else in Scotland as Greer had suggested. But he couldn't do that to his mother and sisters, not when the king would upend their lives to locate Drake. And then there was his honor that he'd spent his entire life establishing, to become a man his da could be proud of.

It was foolish to put such stock in one's pride, but he had assigned such an incredible weight to his morality and the choices he made that they could not be so easily cast aside. Every decision he had made led him to this point. He would now face the consequences.

The ride from the inn to Dunfermline Palace was silent beneath a blanket of tension. Even Mac and Bean quieted as the cart crawled closer to their destination. Drake held the reins with one hand, while the other hand held tightly to Greer, reluctant to let her go. Now or ever.

They were all aware he might be marching to his death. For most of his life, he had lived for the present—a day at a time to put food on the table, to keep a roof over his family's heads, to survive one more day so he could wake up and do it all over again.

Only recently had he put an eye toward the future, with the potentially realized hope of becoming a knight. And then dashing that all away for the woman who had become his wife, a woman he longed to grow old with. He wanted that future back, to spend with Greer, to raise their children as his sisters did now with theirs, in a secure home where he could keep them all safe.

The castle came into view, and Drake's heart slammed against his ribs. Greer tightened her grip on his hand as if she intended to never let go either.

The lads hopped out of the cart and walked slowly alongside, their backs straight and proud. Drake turned back and looked to Bean, hoping the lad would recall the conversation they'd had earlier that morning. Drake had told the lad to disassociate with him, to swear he had tried to convince Drake not to try to rescue Mac from the dungeon. But Bean had refused the offer, saying he had never met a man more honorable than Drake and that, had he known, he would have encouraged Drake's decision.

Now Bean met Drake's gaze directly and gave a single, definitive shake of his head. Still refusing to save himself if he was implicated.

Drake would plead the lad's case for him later with the king.

One of the king's soldiers attached himself to their slow-moving procession toward the castle. Another one did likewise. Within several minutes, as they neared the yawning archway leading to the castle, at least twenty guards were walking alongside the cart as though escorting Drake and his party to the king.

Drake paid them no mind as the cart's wooden wheels clattered over the cobblestones. He stopped in front of the stables, squeezed Greer's hand, and stepped down from the bench, pausing to help his lovely wife down as well.

She caught his eyes, her gaze so wounded in that instant that it cut him to the quick. Leaving her would be his biggest regret. His mother and sisters were safe now, well off with others to help protect them.

But Greer...he would not be there for her any longer. Not when he received his judgment, for the more he mulled over the facts of it all, the more he realized there would likely be no pardon. He had killed an earl. It was an offense that couldn't be forgiven. Even if the king believed Mac's story.

Drake ran his fingers over the back of Greer's hand before letting it go. Her gaze flicked around to the surrounding soldiers, and the emotion in her eyes went as hard as emeralds. The mask he knew she would put up was in place, his bonny, brave lass.

"Beathan," Drake called as though the soldiers were not all standing about him. "See my horse to the stable."

Before Bean could approach the horse, a man with a pale complexion and hair as dark as peat strode toward Drake with an authoritative posture.

Greer stiffened at Drake's side.

The man stopped in front of him. "Master Fletcher, by order of the king, ye are to be taken prisoner for the death of the Earl of Calver. I should hope ye'll do this peacefully."

Drake met the man's small eyes without flinching. "Aye, I will."

A slight relaxing of the man's shoulders reflected his relief that he would not have to use force.

"The lad as well," the man said.

"Nay." Drake stepped forward, encroaching the man's personal space and forcing him to look up, for Drake stood an easy hand-width taller. "The lad took no part in what I did."

"The king—"

"I said, the lad took no part in what I did," Drake repeated, this time in a low, quiet voice.

The guard swallowed and nodded. "I'll speak with the king but be prepared in case we come back for ye." He shot a warning glance at Bean, who nodded solemnly.

"Drake." Greer's soft cry pulled Drake's attention back to her. "My husband."

The guard looked between them. "If she is indeed yer wife, ye may speak to her for a swift moment."

As much as Drake had disliked the shorter man who wielded his authority with limp confidence, he was now grateful for this precious gift.

Though they had said farewell that morning in anticipation of not having this moment, and though Drake ought to decline to ensure he remained strong, he could not turn down this final opportunity to hold his wife one last time.

"Greer." Her name came out in a ragged exhale as emotion choked in his throat. He pulled her into his arms.

She exhaled a shuddering breath against his chest, warm and sweet and reminiscent of the intimacies they had shared the previous night. "I'll talk to the king with Mac," she whispered in a frantic rush. "We'll get ye free."

He knew the likelihood was nearly impossible but also knew she said it more for herself. For hope. For such times truly did require what little one could salvage.

Drake too had hopes for the woman he loved.

"Live a good life," he said. "Go to Skye where I told ye. With my mum—" His voice caught.

"I'll go to Skye with ye," Greer said vehemently, her eyes welling with tears.

She would go alone, and Drake well knew it.

"I love ye." He pressed his mouth to hers before she could offer any further protest. "I will always love ye." He drew away, knowing if he stayed even a moment more, he would never be able to leave.

"Drake." She reached for him. "Wait—"

He shook his head, unable to speak a word more around the growing ache in the back of his throat. He would face his judgment like a man.

But as the guards led him into the keep, he heard her cry out behind him. "I love ye."

It was so raw and so filled with the same emotion burning his chest and digging into his raw, tender heart that he could not stop the moisture from welling in his eyes.

He was truly thankful he was able to bid her farewell and ensure she would indeed live a good life. It was the best gift a man could have before facing his death.

⚜

GREER'S HEART WENT WITH DRAKE AS HE PASSED INTO THE shadowed alcove of the castle and disappeared amid a swarm of soldiers. He would give them no trouble, but of course, they didn't know that. They had no idea of his true sense of honor.

Never had a man existed like Drake Fletcher.

But she was not a woman to stand by and weep at the world's injustices. If she were that type of lass, she wouldn't have made it past ten summers. Nay, she was a woman of grit and determination, one who would survive no matter the cost and protect those she loved.

And she would do everything to ensure Drake was freed. That, and guarantee none of Lord Calver's men came for Mac again. Until he had divulged what he knew to the king, her brother would be in danger of those who wished to see him forever silenced.

She took Mac's hand in hers and marched up to the guards who had closed the space after Drake had left. "I'm Mistress Fletcher, and I demand to see the king."

The guards flicked their gaze over her worn dress, and she knew their answer before they gave it.

"The king doesna see the wives of prisoners," one said with bored disinterest.

She was not so easily dissuaded, though she wouldn't let them know that.

"Verra well," she sighed and turned away from the entrance.

"Greer?" Mac said, confused by how swiftly she'd given up.

"Do ye see Bean?" she asked, skimming the surrounding area.

"There." Mac nodded to a shadowed wall of the castle where Bean leaned against the stone, his expression sullen.

She approached Bean as a plan formed. "I need yer help."

"Anything." The lad straightened. "I'll do whatever it takes to help Drake."

"I was hoping ye'd say that." She exhaled with relief. "Will ye take Mac to yer lodgings in the castle and keep him safe until ye're both summoned by the king?"

"Aye, I can do that." The lads grinned at one another, their fast friendship evident as the two ran off together.

Once they were gone, she found a quiet alcove to slip into and used a bit of linen to bind up her hair like a laundress. If she'd played it successfully at Lochmaben Castle, surely, she could do so again now.

This time, she didn't bother to stop and speak with the guards on her way inside the castle. Instead, she acted as though she knew exactly where she was going as if she belonged there.

As expected, they paid her no mind.

The laundering area of a castle was always located in the depths, where the steam and lye fumes wouldn't cause any unpleasantries to the noble residents upstairs. That familiar sharp odor was an easy one to follow, and within minutes, she strode into the laundry room, which operated in a flurry of activity.

As expected, there was a pile of kirtles nearby, waiting to be brushed out as the accompanying linens were being washed. Greer lifted an elegant green brocade that would become her, one that thankfully laced up at the front and not at the back, as that would be difficult to manage on her own. Next, she took the brush in hand and swept it over the garment to ensure any debris had been removed. After all, such cloth was far too fine to douse with harsh soaps.

Once it was clean, she stood up with a huff. "The mistress said she needs this immediately." She spoke to no one in particular as she quickly strode from the room with the expediency of a servant on an important task. No one bothered to question her.

It was equally as easy to hide in an empty room, one filled with baskets of linens and other various household items. She dressed in the gown and secreted her dusty kirtle in one of the many baskets. The green brocade was a near-perfect fit, save for being slightly too long, but it would do. Falling back on her memory, she braided her hair back in an intricate pattern she'd used to appear more mature when she was younger and slipped from the room with a haughty step.

She was finally ready.

Just as the laundry room had been simple to find, so too was the Great Hall, as it occupied most of the castle's main floor. She stepped through the massive doors, and the room went silent upon her entry. Eyes fixed on her as she crossed the rush-covered floor to where the dais sat to the far right.

"What a lovely lass," someone to her right whispered.

"I have a kirtle nearly exactly like that," came a feminine voice.

Greer quickened her step lest the woman looked too closely and realized it likely *was* her kirtle. The people she passed were not the only ones who stared. So too did the king.

The queen was not at his side, and for that, Greer found herself thankful. Men could be easily manipulated by a skilled woman, especially when they felt another was not watching them.

The guards standing before him followed Greer with their eyes. She stopped before them and offered a confident smile. "I'd like to speak with the king."

One opened his mouth, then closed it, then opened it again.

"Let her through," the king said.

She hesitated by the guard and fluttered her lashes at him. "Would ye be so kind as to summon Beathan?"

The man frowned.

"I believe ye call him Bean," she added as if his informal name were foreign on her tongue.

The man nodded. "Aye, my lady."

Greer let her victorious smile show as she sauntered up to the king and curtseyed the way ladies did. "Yer Majesty."

He was younger than she had expected. Barely above adolescence with a beard upon his chin as though he were trying to add years with its appearance. He grinned at her with a youth's interest when it came to a bonny lass.

"I'm Mistress Fletcher," she said. "Wife of Drake Fletcher, who yer men recently took prisoner."

The king's welcoming demeanor shifted to wariness. "Yer husband killed an earl."

"Lord Calver attacked him." She breathed in and slowly let the air out to steady her racing heart. "I wish to testify against Lord Calver."

"Testify in what manner?" The king lifted a brow, though she didn't know if he was intrigued or merely placating her.

"He was skimming the taxes he owed ye, and he killed Lady Eileen when she threatened to unveil his perfidy."

"What did ye say?" a voice said from somewhere behind Greer.

She glanced over her shoulder to find an older man striding toward her, his face strained. "About Lady Eileen." The guards parted for him, and when he approached, she could see such pain in his eyes that she knew without a shadow of a doubt he must be the dead woman's father.

"Forgive me," she said gently. "But Lord Calver was responsible for Lady Eileen's death."

The man cast a desperate look up to the king, who fixed his attention on Greer. "What proof do ye have of this?"

"A witness," Greer said as she scanned the room in the hope Bean and Mac would make haste. "One Lord Calver had in the dungeon and meant to keep silenced by hanging him."

As if summoned by her desperation, a door to the right opened, and Bean entered with Mac. Greer's brother appeared even younger than his twelve summers from the weeks of starvation in a dank, sunless cell. Already diminutive, he appeared to shrink into himself at the attention of so many eyes.

"He's just a bairn." The king waved Mac over and addressed him directly. "Ye were placed in the dungeon for what ye saw?"

Mac looked around him, his eyes enormous in his small face as he took in how many people were attentively watching him.

"Leave us." The king's command was given with such volume that it echoed from the stone walls.

The room cleared at once, so only the king, Mac and Greer remained. And Lord Androll.

Greer had moved to depart as well, but the king held up his hand to indicate she should stay.

The king leaned forward in his chair and peered at Mac. "Did ye see Lord Calver kill Lady Eileen?"

Mac nodded. "Aye, yer majesty."

"What was she wearing?" Lord Androll demanded.

Mac squinted in the distance as he appeared to call upon his memory. "A pink kirtle and a necklace with pink stones."

The color drained from Lord Androll's face at hearing proof that Mac had seen his daughter on her last day alive. He nodded at King David, who nodded toward Mac. "Tell us exactly what happened."

"I saw them in the clearing in the woods that day," Mac replied earnestly. "She said he was committing treason, that he wasn't giving the king the full taxes, and she knew about it, that she would tell. He told her to mind herself, but she wouldna stop talking about how he was stealing from the crown. Before she could finish what she had to say, his face went the color of roasted pig, and he ran at her, hitting her with his fists and screaming like a madman." Mac's lips twisted slightly as he paused. "I was hiding behind a tree until then and ran out when I saw him hit her. But before I could get to her, he struck her with such force that her head turned to the side. She dropped to the ground, and dinna get back up. The way she fell like that, I knew I couldna help anymore."

Mac stared off in the distance as he spoke, his gaze haunted by what he'd witnessed.

"'Twas brave of ye to try," the king offered.

Mac blinked at the words and jerked his attention to the king. "I suppose it was..." The left toe of his shoe dug into the rushes at his feet in his bashful acceptance of the compliment.

The king lifted his brows. "And that's when the earl saw ye."

"Aye. Lord Calver shoved at her, so she rolled down the hill, and that's when he saw me. I tried to hide, but his guards came after me later, capturing me." Mac shifted his weight from one foot to the other. "They wouldna tell me what I'd done wrong or let me out. They wouldna even get notice to my sister—" He paused and sniffled.

Greer's heart clenched at how terrified he must have been— confused and alone in that dark, terrible cell.

"Thank ye for sharing this," the king said in a grave voice.

Mac nodded and twisted the toe of his worn shoe into the rushes once more.

The king kept his face impassive as he dismissed them. As Greer was leading Mac from the room, the king asked the guards to bring up the prisoner.

The strength in her legs bled away, and she nearly collapsed at the implication of that order. She only hoped that Mac had shared enough and the king had believed him.

Drake's life depended on it.

❧ 23 ❧

"The king wants to see ye."

The gruff voice pulled Drake from his contemplation. His thoughts sped tenfold as the door to his cell opened. This might be his only chance to stand before the king and give his defense. There had to be some way of getting out of his predicament.

The Great Hall had been cleared of all occupants save the king, Lord Androll and two guards on either side of them.

"Drake Fletcher, ye stand accused of killing Lord Calver." The young king curled his fingers over the arms of his carved chair. "What say ye?"

"I should like to start by stating that Beathan MacKenzie dinna have a hand in any of it and was ignorant of my actions." Drake widened his stance, determined to fight for his freedom with honor, to rely on justice and protect those he could. "'Twas my blade that sliced Lord Calver's skin, aye, but the slice was unintentional. He was attacking me, and I moved to evade his blow. I lowered my sword to avoid causing harm at the exact moment he lunged. There are leg wounds in battle sometimes—"

The king put up his hand to stop Drake. "Did he attack ye

first?"

"He attacked a bairn and my wife first. I couldna stand by and see them injured, so I defended them." Drake gave a respectful nod toward Lord Androll. "The lad had information about Lady Eileen's death. Something Lord Calver dinna want to get out."

"We know." The king narrowed his eyes. "Why did ye come here?"

Drake frowned. "I beg yer pardon, sire?"

"Ye knew ye had slain a nobleman, yet still ye came to Dunfermline Palace, though surely ye were aware an army would be waiting for ye." The king's dark gaze fixed on Drake.

"I did know that," Drake acquiesced. "But I regret none of my decisions."

The king's auburn brows lifted in surprise. "How so?"

"I'm no' the type of man to run," Drake said. "I dinna regret my choice to rescue the lad from the dungeon. He shouldna have been there at all and would have hanged were he no' freed. Rescuing him was the honorable thing to do. As was coming here to fulfill my mission."

"Ye returned knowing ye would likely be taken to the dungeon, just so ye could complete the task we sent ye on?"

Drake nodded firmly. "Aye, my liege. The lad has information concerning the death of Lord Androll's daughter I thought ye ought to know."

The king nodded. "We're well aware."

Then Greer had already managed to get an audience for Mac to speak to the king.

"The lad has been verra brave." Drake might have chains on his wrists, but it would not stop him from asking for the boy's protection. "There are many who would see him harmed for what he knows. I beg of ye to ensure he remains safe."

The corner of the king's mouth quirked upward. "Ye plead for the life of another, even as ye stand before us accused of the murder of a nobleman."

Drake didn't cower from such words spoken by the king. "Mac is an innocent with unfortunate timing."

The king pushed up from his chair and slowly made his way down the three stairs. Lord Androll said nothing but remained in place, simply watching.

Drake's heartbeat echoed in his ears, but he refused to show any emotion.

The king gazed up at him. Up close, Scotland's monarch appeared even younger than he did from a distance, his face as smooth and unlined as a bairn's beneath his short beard. "Ye truly are an honorable man."

His words took Drake aback.

"Ye did exactly as we asked ye," the king continued. "At risk to yer own freedom, and ye dinna once plea for yerself, but only for those ye meant to protect. Those who warrant protection given their age and innocence." He nodded slightly to himself. "We recall yer da was a knight. They say 'tis why ye wish to be one as well."

The very mention of Drake's father crushed at his chest. He nodded, unsure how to even respond to such a devastating reminder.

"We believe," the younger man said, "we believe yer father would be verra proud of what ye've done."

Proud?

Drake tilted his head, unsure he had heard correctly.

"We canna think of a single man who would return to face certain capture to fulfill their duty." The king gave a broad smile and patted Drake on the shoulder. "We exonerate ye from blame relating to the death of the Earl of Calver."

Drake exhaled, unable to stifle his shock.

"And as for becoming a knight..." The king summoned a guard and indicated Drake's manacles. "Ye fulfilled yer end of the agreement."

The guard stepped forward and unlocked the manacles from

Drake's wrists, releasing their leaden weight from his arms.

"We will now fulfill ours." The king smiled. "We will see ye knighted as soon as a feast can be prepared."

The change of events had Drake reeling. He had come to the Great Hall expecting to be charged with murdering an earl and being sentenced to death. Never had he dreamed of being still considered for knighthood.

"Thank ye," he whispered. The emotion and gratitude overwhelmed him, leaving him bereft of anything more to say.

"Thank yer wife." The king waved his hand toward a guard, who opened the door. "Her tenacity in meeting with us proved yer innocence, which ye confirmed with yer answers, all of which have been supported by other men who were there as well."

Greer ran through the now-open doorway, not stopping as she raced over the rushes toward him. She wore a green brocade gown, with her lustrous auburn hair pulled back from her face in a series of braids. Her skin was like cream against the fabric, and her eyes shone brilliantly as emeralds.

She looked every bit a noblewoman.

Drake nearly asked where she'd gotten the kirtle but then realized the answer was most likely not one best witnessed by the king.

"My husband." She threw herself into his arms.

He wrapped her in his arms, savoring the familiar curves of her body and the sweet, floral scent he feared he would never breathe in again. "I'm free," he said against her silky hair. "Thanks to ye."

"More than free," the king added. "He's to become a knight."

She blinked up at Drake, tears welling in her eyes. "What's happened?"

"I'll tell ye in detail." He embraced her again and whispered into her ear, "After we celebrate."

THE FEAST FOR DRAKE'S KNIGHTING CELEBRATION WAS prepared within two days. While Greer reluctantly had to return the green kirtle to the laundry, she was able to procure a lovely emerald-colored gown to match Drake's new tunic.

She entered the Great Hall, which had been laid out with flowers adorning the tables and fine pewter bowls of food and flagons filled with rich, luxurious wine. She and Mac were shown to a table of honor beside the king, where Bean was already sitting with a wide smile on his face.

Drake entered the room, and all conversation stopped. Greer's heart swelled to see her handsome husband as he strode confidently toward the dais, his back straight, shoulders squared. She knew exactly how long he had wanted this, as well as what he had done to earn it.

Most especially, she knew what this meant to him—a legacy made whole, knowing his father would have been so incredibly proud.

He knelt before the king, who lightly touched the flat of a gleaming blade first to one of Drake's shoulders, then the other. It was then that Drake swore his oath of fealty in a clear, even voice, the timbre of it echoing from the high rafters. The king presented Drake with the coveted golden spurs of a knight and a noble sword fashioned specifically for him.

And it was done.

Drake was a knight.

After spending so much of his life struggling in ways that Greer knew all too well, after rising high with the English and falling low to save his sister from certain death, after thinking he was to lose his life for the sake of honor—finally, he was knighted.

Tears clogged her throat when he approached the dais where she sat. He knelt before her and took her hand, bringing it to his lips. As he did so, his gaze held hers, filled with such love that her heart felt as though it could scarcely fit in her chest.

"I'm so proud of ye," she whispered.

"I couldna have done it without ye, my bonny wife." He got to his feet and settled into the chair beside her, pausing to grin at Mac, who beamed at him with the same admiration as Bean did.

Drake sliced off the best part of the venison before them and slid it onto the plate in front of Greer. "Before the ceremony began, the king came to me and said he had approved my post on Skye."

Eagerness charged through Greer. They had discussed the idea of moving away from the border to the Isle of Skye where his family was, and he could ensure her and Mac's care when he was called to his purpose. Where it would be safe.

"There is a manor near Dunscaith Castle he has given us as a wedding present." Drake let his hand graze hers as he reached for a roll. "And made a point to state it is an ideal place for bairns."

"Then we shall have to consider growing our family." Greer slid him a smile.

"My da is here." Bean leapt up from the table abruptly. "My da is here. He came."

Mac jumped from his seat and joined Bean as they dashed across the room to where a tall man with silver hair greeted them both.

"It appears we'll be finally meeting Bean's da after all we've heard about him," Greer said, smiling at the lad's enthusiasm as she pushed up from her seat along with Drake.

The man followed the eager boys back to the dais and inclined his head to Greer and Drake with a grin reminiscent of Bean's. His eyes were the same brilliant blue as well. While Greer did not know what the lad's mother looked like, he evidently favored his da.

"I've no' ever seen my lad so excited," the man said. "Felicitations, Sir Drake." He locked arms with him. "And Lady Fletcher."

It was strange to be treated with such deference after a lifetime of being little more than a vagrant, yet it was a shift Greer could easily get used to.

"Well met..." Drake paused so that the man might give his name.

"Duncan MacKenzie." He inclined his head again.

Drake straightened. Greer glanced at him to ascertain why he had such a curious reaction and found her husband's gaze on the hilt of a dagger near the man's hip, where a small golden rose had been etched.

"Duncan MacKenzie," Drake repeated.

"Aye." The man's smile widened.

"I believe ye may know my mother." Drake paused a moment before saying her name, "Cait Ross."

The muscles of Duncan's neck stood out as he sucked in a hard breath. "Cait?"

"Are ye the Duncan MacKenzie I think ye to be?" Drake asked. "The one she loved in her youth?"

"She wasna the only one in love." Duncan's affable expression took on a sad note. "I pray she is still well."

"She is," Drake replied. "She was widowed when I was a lad and now lives on Skye with my sisters and their bairns."

"Widowed?" Duncan swallowed. "I'm sorry to hear it."

But he did not look so terribly sorry to hear it.

"I too am a widower," he replied. "My wife did not survive Beathan's birth."

"We are venturing to Skye soon," Greer interjected. "Mayhap ye might join us. To see where Bean will be staying now that he has officially become Drake's squire."

Duncan nodded. "Aye, I'd like that."

"Ye're going to join us on Skye?" Bean asked, bouncing on the balls of his feet. "What a grand adventure."

"Indeed, it will be." Drake helped Greer to her chair once more before taking his own.

"Yer mother was in love with him?" Greer asked as her eyes followed Bean and his father as they took their seats on the opposite side of the table.

"She thought my grandda had him killed." Drake lifted his brows. "I imagine it will be quite a surprise to her to find him still alive."

Greer slid a bit of venison into her mouth and thought as she chewed, imagining what it would be like to be separated for years from Drake, to presume him dead only to find him alive and themselves both widowed. "I imagine she will be most pleased."

"Aye, we have much to look forward to upon our arrival at our new home." Drake covered her hand with his and gazed tenderly down at her, a silent promise for the life they would live together, the one that had seemed little more than a fantasy only days before.

September 1342
Isle of Skye

THE JOURNEY TO DUNSCAITH CASTLE HAD BEEN TIME consuming to keep the exertion of travel from being too taxing on Greer or Mac. Though they both insisted they were fully recovered, Drake wanted to ensure Greer's injury did not fester again, and that Mac continued to build his strength after his time in the dungeon.

Additionally, Drake had wanted to allow them to gather what they wanted from their cottage by Lochmaben, as well as collect Bean's horse, Brevis, who made the journey as well as any hearty destrier.

The welcome they received was entirely worth the duration of the journey.

Drake's brother-in-law, Reid, was the captain of the guard at Dunscaith Castle and the first to see them.

"We wondered when ye might finally arrive," he called jovially down as the drawbridge lowered to allow them entry.

Reid acted quickly in notifying the Fletcher family, and by the time Drake, Greer and the rest of their party had arrived in the courtyard, his family was pouring out from the keep's entryway.

Sir William, castellan of the keep and husband to Drake's youngest sister, Kinsey, approached them with open arms. "Welcome to Dunscaith Castle, Sir Drake. And I take it ye're the bonny Lady Fletcher."

Kinsey appeared at her husband's side with a beaming smile. "Ach, I dinna ever think Drake would find a lass who could finally steal his heart." She whispered loudly to Drake, "And she's so bonny as well."

She laughed as Drake caught her in an embrace.

"She is bonny," said Faye, the eldest of the three sisters, as she bounced a chubby babe on her hip. "Though I'm sure ye're especially partial to her auburn hair." She gently tweaked one of Kinsey's bright red curls and grinned at her.

"I'm Clara." Drake's middle sister stepped forward and warmly embraced his wife. The action was somewhat awkward because of her belly, now large and round with a bairn they were soon expecting. "Ye must be Greer. We've heard such wonderful things about ye in Drake's missives."

A flush colored Greer's cheeks. "I'm sure, from a man with a biased opinion." She laughed and glanced at Drake.

His heart missed the next beat, the same as it always did when their eyes connected, and their souls brushed in those moments. God, how he loved his wife, and how proud he was for his sisters to finally meet her.

"This is Faye and her husband Ewan," Clara said.

Ewan appeared beside Faye and lifted wee Callum from her arms, earning him an endearing kiss.

"Then Kinsey and her husband Sir William," Clara continued, indicating where the two stood side by side, their fingers entwined.

"And this is my husband, Reid." Clara waved a hand to her

husband, who joined her, wrapping his arms around her, and resting his hands protectively over her round belly.

"And this is Elspeth or Kieran," Reid added, indicating her swollen abdomen.

Everyone gave a little laugh as the remainder of the introductions went around, first to Mac and then to Bean as Drake's new squire, but as they got to Duncan, two more figures filled the entrance of the castle and came out into the courtyard.

Drake's mother and his grandda, the cantankerous Chieftain of the Ross clan. Whatever Ross was saying to Mum had put a slight frown on her face.

"And this is..." Drake said, trying to gain his mother's attention.

Indeed, he had it in a fraction of a moment. Mum stopped abruptly, and her hand flew to the base of the throat. "Duncan."

Duncan MacKenzie stepped forward, his eyes burning with emotion. "Cait."

"I thought ye were dead." Mum turned to Drake's grandda. "I thought ye had him killed."

Ross scoffed. "Even I need a better reason than that to kill someone. I had them beat his arse and told him he'd give ye nothing but a lifetime of misery with the constant war between our people. I dinna want ye to have a life where ye always felt as though ye were hiding."

"I knew he was right, and dinna want to ruin yer life," Duncan stepped forward.

"Ye wouldna have." Mum's eyes filled with tears. "I wanted to be with ye no matter what that meant."

"I was only trying to protect ye, Cait," Ross said gently.

She glared at her father and went to Duncan. "Welcome to Dunscaith Castle. I implore ye to stay as long as ye like. And yer wife..." Her gaze discreetly moved over the courtyard.

"My mum died when I was born," Bean offered. "I'm his son, Beathan."

"Beathan, well met." Mum's smile grew a little wider, and she turned to Greer. "Ach, and ye must be Greer. Ye've got the face of an angel, lass." She embraced Drake's wife and grinned in his direction, a clear sign she already loved her new daughter-in-law.

Once Drake and Greer were settled in their rooms in the castle, they had horses readied to ride out to their manor. Mum was still in the courtyard, locked in deep conversation with Duncan, the rose brooch that had been so significant all those years ago pinned to her bodice. With the MacKenzies and the Rosses at peace with one another finally, no one opposed or begrudged their quiet reunion.

Drake and Greer did not disturb the two as they mounted their horses and left Dunscaith Castle for the stone manor that sat on its outskirts. The structure was a tower house atop a craggy ridge. The home rose three stories and required a drawbridge to enter it over a deep ravine. It was a house that would promise safety.

There were only a few guards on hand, one of which lowered the drawbridge and bade them welcome.

"'Tis lovely," Greer breathed, looking up at the side of the keep with its many sea-facing windows.

"Would ye like to go inside?" Drake drew her toward him and pressed a kiss to her silky auburn hair.

"Aye," she said, still craning her neck in awe.

The guard rushed to open the door for them. The creak echoed through the empty entryway, as did the thunderous boom of it closing as he left them alone to explore.

"Once it's filled with furnishings, it willna echo so much," Drake said.

"It's more than I ever dreamed I would live in." She curled her arm around him. "With a man that I dinna ever dare to imagine existed."

He stroked his hand down her cheek. "I waited for ye for a long time, lass."

"And thanks be to God for it." She kissed him.

But before they could lose themselves in one another, he brought her through the home to explore. First to their own Great Hall, which was large enough to host at least fifty people, then to the chamber where they would sleep together.

"And where does this lead?" She asked about the stairs going up from their bedchamber.

"Let's find out." He guided her up the curling stone staircase, his hand at the slight dip of her lower back where he loved to trace delicately upward and watch her shiver in delight.

The stairs ended in a small room with a cradle set in one corner.

"A nursery," Drake said proudly. "Close enough to where we are to keep an eye on the bairn."

"And a good thing too." Greer slid a sly grin up at him. "Remember how ye worried we might have conceived the night we lay together?"

Drake's heartbeat kicked faster in his chest. "Aye?"

"I missed my courses." Greer's eyes danced with delight. "'Tis been over a fortnight, but I dinna want to say until I thought I could be certain."

"Ye're with child?" he asked, incredulous at his good fortune.

She laughed and nodded. He pulled her into his arms and spun her about.

His had not been an easy life, but he would endure it all again for even a taste of what he now had. The knighthood he had always wanted, the woman he had never thought existed, and the brilliantly happy future he never dreamed would belong to him.

A tear slipped down Greer's cheek.

He wiped it away, concerned suddenly. "What is it, my love?"

She shook her head, smiling. "I'm so verra happy, Drake."

He pulled her into his arms, breathing in her light floral scent, relishing the joy of his incredible life. "So am I, my wife. So am I."

EPILOGUE

August 1344
Isle of Skye

Dunscaith Castle was filled to the brim with people and bustling with activity. Of course, it wasn't every day a wedding took place. Especially not one that had taken decades to finally happen.

Drake guided Greer inside the keep while Mac and Bean secured the horses in the stable and ran off some energy before having to sit on the hardback pews for the ceremony.

Kinsey rushed by and thrust something into Drake's hands. "Bring this to Mum." Without so much as a greeting, she waddled off toward the kitchens, cradling the bump of her burgeoning belly.

He looked down at the small rose brooch in his hand, the one that had been the symbol of the love between his mother and Duncan for so long.

"We knew it would be madness." Greer grinned at Drake and propped their son, Malcolm, onto her hip. The lad squirmed about, eager to run about but not yet skilled enough to do so effectively without eventually getting hurt.

"Down," he pleaded.

"Greer?" Faye called out from somewhere unseen. "I need ye in here."

Greer lifted her brows in amusement.

"I'll take him to see his grandmum." Drake pulled their son from Greer's arms, where he proceeded to wriggle with ceaseless energy in Drake's firm grasp.

"Best of luck to ye." Greer kissed Malcolm's chubby cheek, then looked to Drake. Her green eyes searched his for a brief moment in that soul-catching way she had. "I love ye, Drake Fletcher. I'll see ye at the chapel."

He kissed her, still relishing the softness of her sweet lips on his after two years of being wed, and off she went toward a fresh cry of panic from Faye.

Laughing, Drake set Malcolm to his feet and held the lad's chubby hand as the bairn toddled at a snail's pace toward Mum's chamber. When they arrived, she answered the door in a blue silk gown that made her eyes look as blue as the deepest ocean. She gave a giddy laugh when she saw Malcolm and lifted him into her arms, much to the lad's delight, for he gave a great squeal and clapped his hands.

"Kinsey thought ye might need this." Drake handed her the brooch.

She propped Malcolm on her hip and took the brooch. "Ach, how could I have forgotten?"

"'Tis a bit mad here today." Drake made a face, and his mother laughed.

She studied him with a peculiar smile on her face. "Ye're no' as tense as ye always used to be, do ye know that?"

He tilted his head.

His mother smiled. "Yer Greer is good for ye. Ye've spent too long being so serious, walking through life in a rigid line. She's shown ye how to venture off the path, and ye're a better man for it."

Malcolm reached for the brooch, but she pulled it away. "And ye make fine babies." She laughed and handed the bairn back to Drake.

It was true what she said. Drake still upheld his intention to be an honorable knight, but he did not fall back on the same pedantic stoicism as he had before. Life was more enjoyable, lighthearted, and fun. And he knew Greer and her antics had everything to do with it. That and Malcolm's endless energy and the kind, playful way Mac always handled the wee lad.

"I thought there was to be a wedding?" boomed a voice from below.

Mum chuckled. "It would appear yer grandda has arrived."

In the last two years, much had changed as Faye continued to visit with Ewan and their son, Callum, and Clara and Reid's daughter, Elspeth, was born. The Chieftain of the Ross clan came to Dunscaith more often, with gifts and smiles that became less rare as his great-grandchildren warmed the chill of his icy heart.

And in that time, so too did Drake's mother soften toward her father, seeing that he truly had meant to protect her in the best way he knew how. Especially when she realized that in trying to protect her own children from him, she had made their life harder than was necessary. It was an understanding that left her bereft for some time but eventually helped facilitate the renewed love for her once-estranged father.

"I think that means we are late." Drake shifted Malcolm into his arms to kiss his dark, glossy hair. "Let's go find yer mum, aye?"

"Mum," his son exclaimed, his eyes alight with eager anticipation.

As suspected, the chaos of the castle had gone still as everyone piled into the small chapel. It was crowded within, the pews filled with families that were healthy, happy, and safe.

Clara and Reid were in one row with Elspeth settled between them. The lass's hair was auburn like her da's, and the lass had the same gentle, patient spirit as her mum.

Faye and Ewan were in another row, his arm around her shoulders as wee Callum kicked his feet out from the bench repeatedly until Ewan put a hand to the lad's head, stilling the motion.

In yet another pew were Kinsey and William, their hands together resting on the bump of her belly where their first child grew.

Greer sat on another bench with Bean and Mac beside her, both lads grinning in anticipation of the day Bean's da would wed Mac's adopted grandmum, strange though it might sound when the couple was nearly the same age. Drake approached his family's pew, and Greer reached up for Malcolm, who nestled into her arms and rubbed at his eyes.

Drake sank onto the seat beside his wife and put his arm around her so she could lean against him as she cradled the weight of their groggy son. She smiled up at him, love shining in her eyes.

"Ye make me so verra happy," he whispered to her.

"We are so verra happy," she said in agreement and nuzzled closer so he could smell the sweet perfume of her hair.

The doors to the chapel opened, and Mum appeared, her eyes alight with excitement as Duncan turned where he stood at the altar and broke into a wide smile. Finally, their love would result in the union that should have been nearly three decades ago.

Drake's da was a good man who had cared for them all, and truly Mum had loved him. She'd told Drake she was grateful to have met and wed her first husband, to have the children she had. Their family was one Mum wouldn't change for the world.

Aye, it was a struggle sometimes, but in the end, it had all worked out with Mum and Duncan rediscovering their love, with all of Drake's sisters married to men who treated them with respect and adoration, with a knighthood Drake had never thought attainable.

And with a beautiful wife that kept his life interesting in the best possible ways.

Indeed, their lives had flourished in these years, and it warmed his heart to know that all were so content. For truly, life had a fascinating way of working out. And there was nothing better in life than finding happiness in love.

Thank you for reading DRAKE'S HONOR! I read all of my reviews and would love to know that you enjoyed it, so please do leave a review.

Drake's siblings all have their own stories too:

- Faye in *Faye's Sacrifice*
- Kinsey in *Kinsey's Defiance*
- Clara in *Clara's Vow*
- You can also find Anice's story, book 2 of my Borderland Ladies here in *Anice's Bargain*
- If you want more stories that take place on the border between England and Scotland (and get even more Drake!), check out my Borderland Ladies series, starting with *Marin's Promise*

THIS OFFICIALLY CONCLUDES MY BORDERLAND LADIES AND Borderland Rebels series, though I have many more historical romance (as well as historical fiction) you can check out - please go to http://www.madelinemartin.com for more.

Sign up for my exclusive newsletter to stay up to date on the latest book news and receive a FREE book download
www.MadelineMartin/newsletter

AUTHOR'S NOTE

Laundry is a deplorable task in the 21st century, but even more so in the 1300s! Generally most people washed their clothes about once a month due to how time consuming it was, or they could hire someone like Greer who would take in laundry to wash for other people.

The edges of the lochs were the best place for washing with having water constantly available as much was needed when it came to scrubbing soiled garments. The main method of cleaning was using lye, though eventually something called soapwort was used as well. Soapwort was a plant that exuded a soap-like consistency that was perfect for cleaning and being gentle on clothing, although it wasn't hugely popular until the 16th century. The construction of lye soap was a little gross – it was water run through with ashes and made into soap using animal fat. It wasn't uncommon for urine to be added as well as a whitening agent (which, yes, actually worked). This was not a bar of soap as you would use today, but a soft, runny texture.

Not all garments could be easily washed, however. Fine cloth had to generally only be soaked in warm, scented water occasionally, but generally after each wear, the gown was brushed clean of debris. This was why wearing linens was so popular as the linens could be washed often and often protected the garment from body oils/smells, etc.

The job of a laundress was not easy and required a considerable amount of strength not only to haul the buckets and baskets of laundry, but also using a bat-like thing or a paddle to beat the clothing or even a scrubbing board to ensure all stains were removed after a good lye-soaking.

So, the next time you bemoan having to do a few loads of laundry, just remember how much worse it really could be. I know I'm a lot more grateful for my washer and dryer after all this research!

ACKNOWLEDGMENTS

THANK YOU TO my amazing beta readers who helped make this story so much more with their wonderful suggestions: Tracy Emro and Tina Ullrich. You ladies are so amazing and make my books just shine!

Thank you to Erica Monroe with Quillfire Author Services for the consistently amazing edits.

Thank you to Janet Kazmirski for the final read-through you always do for me and for catching all the little last minute tweaks.

Thank you to John and my wonderful minions for all the support they give me. And to Ink for sitting in my lap and keeping me on task (mostly).

And a huge thank you so much to my readers for always being so fantastically supportive and eager for my next book.

ABOUT THE AUTHOR

Madeline Martin is a New York Times and International Bestselling author of historical fiction and historical romance.

She lives in sunny Florida with her two daughters (known collectively as the minions), one incredibly spoiled cat and a man so wonderful he's been dubbed Mr. Awesome. She is a die-hard history lover who will happily lose herself in research any day. When she's not writing, researching or 'moming', you can find her spending time with her family at Disney or sneaking a couple spoonfuls of Nutella while laughing over cat videos. She also loves to travel, attributing her fascination with history to having spent most of her childhood as an Army brat in Germany.

Find out more about Madeline at her website:

http://www.madelinemartin.com

 facebook.com/MadelineMartinAuthor
 twitter.com/MadelineMMartin
 instagram.com/madelinemmartin
 bookbub.com/profile/madeline-martin
amazon.com/Madeline-Martin/e/B00R8OGFN2/ref=ntt_athr_dp_pel_1

REGENCY NOVELLAS (MATCHMAKER OF MAYFAIR)

Discovering the Duke

Unmasking the Earl (A Midsummer Night's Romance Anthology)

Mesmerizing the Marquis

Earl of Benton (Wicked Earls' Club)

Earl of Oakhurst (Wicked Earls' Club)

Earl of Kendal (Wicked Earls' Club)

MEDIEVAL NOVELLAS

The Highlander's Challenge

The Highlander's Lady Knight

Her Highland Beast

HARLEQUIN HISTORICALS

How to Tempt a Duke

How to Start a Scandal

How to Wed a Courtesan

HIGHLAND PASSIONS

A Ghostly Tale of Forbidden Love

The Madam's Highlander

The Highlander's Untamed Lady

Her Highland Destiny

Highland Passions Box Set Volume 1

WWII HISTORICAL FICTION

The Last Bookshop in London

HEART OF THE HIGHLANDS

Deception of a Highlander

Possession of a Highlander

Enchantment of a Highlander

THE MERCENARY MAIDENS

Highland Spy

Highland Ruse

Highland Wrath

Manufactured by Amazon.ca
Bolton, ON